Thirteen

Thirteen

Lauren Myracle

DUTTON CHILDREN'S BOOKS

DUTTON CHILDREN'S BOOKS • A division of Penguin Young Readers Group
Published by the Penguin Group
Penguin Group (USA) Inc., 375 Hudson Street, New York, New York 10014, U.S.A.
Penguin Group (Canada), 90 Eglinton Avenue East, Suite 700, Toronto, Ontario, Canada M4P 2Y3 (a division of Pearson Penguin Canada Inc.) • Penguin Books Ltd, 80 Strand, London WC2R 0RL, England • Penguin Ireland, 25 St Stephen's Green, Dublin 2, Ireland (a division of Penguin Books Ltd) • Penguin Group (Australia), 250 Camberwell Road, Camberwell, Victoria 3124, Australia (a division of Pearson Australia Group Pty Ltd) • Penguin Books India Pvt Ltd, 11 Community Centre, Panchsheel Park, New Delhi–110 017, India • Penguin Group (NZ), 67 Apollo Drive, Rosedale, North Shore 0632, New Zealand (a division of Pearson New Zealand Ltd) • Penguin Books (South Africa) (Pty) Ltd, 24 Sturdee Avenue, Rosebank, Johannesburg 2196, South Africa
Penguin Books Ltd, Registered Offices: 80 Strand, London WC2R 0RL, England

Library of Congress Cataloging-in-Publication Data

Myracle, Lauren, date.
Thirteen / by Lauren Myracle.
p. cm.
Summary: Winnie's thirteenth year brings many joys and challenges as she negotiates her relationship with her first boyfriend and realizes that change is inevitable in her friends, family, and even herself.

ISBN: 978-0-525-47896-6 (hardcover)
[1. Interpersonal relations—Fiction. 2. Friendship—Fiction. 3. Family life—Atlanta (Ga.)—Fiction. 4. Schools—Fiction. 5. Atlanta (Ga.)—Fiction.] I. Title.
PZ7.M9955Td 2008
[Fic]—dc22 2007017213

Published in the United States by Dutton Children's Books,
a division of Penguin Young Readers Group
345 Hudson Street, New York, New York 10014
www.penguin.com/youngreaders

Designed by IRENE VANDERVOORT

Printed in USA First Edition

10 9 8 7 6

For every girl
who's trying to be her best, truest self.
I believe in you!

Acknowledgments

Special thankies to all the girls who've written or e-mailed with tales of their own lives. I'm so honored that y'all share that stuff with me. Thanks to Jim Shuler for medical advice—though, if I got anything wrong, blame me. Thanks to Amber and Julia for making it possible for me to find time to write, and thanks to the lovely baristas at the Starbucks on Drake and Shields for providing such a warm and welcoming "office." Thanks to my mom and sis for reading the first draft and telling me they liked it. A *big* thanks to Anne Havard (from Westminster!) for keeping me straight on all sorts of things. Thanks to my agent, Barry Goldblatt, who handles boring business-y details with humor and finesse, and who's never too busy to talk about the important stuff as well. Thanks to Beegee Tolpa, who captures Winnie perfectly with her art. (Oh good heavens, her illustrations are so fab, aren't they?) Thank you, thank you, thank you to all the wonderful Dutton folks for giving my books such a happy home, and a squillion more thanks to the wonderful Julie Strauss-Gabel, who has a keen eye and a kind heart and whom we should all bow down and praise. Together now, kids: *Yaaaaaaaay, Julie!* And of course, forever and ever, thanks and hugs and kisses to my sweet, goofy family. Without you, I would be a dried-up Fig Newton, crusty and alone.

Thirteen

March

THE THING ABOUT BIRTHDAYS, especially if you just that very day turned thirteen, is that you should know in your heart of hearts that the world is your oyster. Even if you don't like oysters, because of the slime factor. And because they're gray. And have no eyes. Eating an oyster is like swallowing a fishy blob of Jell-O, and frankly, I'm not a fan. I would not, however, run away shrieking if someone dangled an oyster in front of me, like my BFF, Dinah, would.

Last year on my birthday, I snuck home a shrimp from Benihana, because in addition to being anti-oyster, Dinah is also possessed of a shrimp phobia, the poor dear. I waited until just the right moment, then whipped out the shrimp and jiggled it in front of her, making scary shrimp *I'm-going-to-get-you* noises. There was shrieking. There was cat fur. There was an extremely irate older sister—that would be Sandra—who huffed off with her tub of shrimp-juice-tainted mud mask, which Dinah and I had kind of borrowed.

Ah, the good ol' days.

But today is a good day, too, because today I turned thirteen. It is big, and that bigness hummed inside me even though I tried to play it cool when first Mom and Dad, and then my friends at school, made the obligatory "Ooo, a teenager at last" sort of comments. Dorky, dorky, dorky.

And yet, there's truth behind the dorkiness. I will never be a "child" again. People might call me a child. In fact, I'm sure they will, and I'll glare at them hormonally. But my childhood days are over. There's a Bible verse Grandmom Perry made me learn . . . what was it? *When I was a child, I spoke as a child, I understood as a child, I thought as a child. But now that I am grown, I have put away such childish things.*

It has a tinge of sadness to it, despite the glory of my slumber-party-to-come, complete with Bobbi Brown makeovers at the mall. Growing up is always tinged with sadness; that's what I was coming to learn. You got boobs, but you also got zits. You got to wear cooler clothes, but you felt self-conscious when people noticed you in them. You realized your parents weren't perfect and amazing and all-powerful, which was liberating in a way, but, well, you also realized your parents weren't perfect and amazing and all-powerful. Which sucked. As a little kid, I thought my parents had all the answers. As I got older, I realized no one did.

And let's not forget the friend thing. Back in the olden days, it was all so easy. Take my little brother, Ty, for example. He's six, and he's friends with everyone, even the kids he doesn't like. I went with Mom to pick him up from school last week (because Westminster, where I go, had a teacher workday, and Trinity, Ty's elementary school, didn't), and I saw this kid reach over and pinch Ty on his side. The kid laughed after he did it, and not in a nice way.

"Who was that who pinched you?" I asked him after he climbed into the backseat.

"Gary," Ty said.

"*Why* did he pinch you?"

"Because he has sharp fingernails. And because he wants me to think he's a snake, because I'm scared of snakes."

"What a jerk," I said.

"Winnie," Mom warned.

"Fine, he was *acting* like a jerk," I said. Mom was okay with that, with our saying that someone was *acting* jerky or stupid or annoying. She just didn't want us saying someone *was* a jerk. My opinion was that Mom was *acting* naïve to think that made any difference. "Anyway, a snakebite wouldn't feel like a pinch."

"What would it feel like?" Ty asked.

"I don't know. Not a pinch."

"A stabbing pain of hot lava?"

"And it wouldn't be on your waist, either, unless the snake slithered up your pants."

"Winnie!" Mom said.

"It wouldn't," I said. "And I don't like Gary for doing that."

"Me neither," Ty said. "He should go to the juvenile detention center."

"Maybe you should stand in the pick-up line with someone else," I suggested. "One of your friends, and not Gary."

Ty had looked puzzled.

"Gary *is* my friend," he said, as if he were explaining some basic fact.

In seventh grade, if someone pinched you hard enough to bring tears to your eyes, you wouldn't stay friends with them. Only instead of pinching, a seventh grader was more likely to be snakelike in other ways, like whispering to someone that you were "trying too hard" if you wore pink eye shadow. Or that your shirt was too tight. Or too loose. Or that you really needed to clip your toenails if you didn't want to gross everybody out.

So as a seventh grader, no, you weren't friends with people you didn't like. But sometimes you also weren't friends with people you *did* like, which was complicated, and which didn't make sense if you tried to explain it. Sometimes things just changed. That's where the sadness came in.

I can't really complain, though. Dinah is my BFF number one; Cinnamon is my BFF number two. Plenty of people have more than one best-friend-forevers. That's allowed. And my ex-BFF is Amanda.

On the very extremely plus side of being thirteen, I also have a—yikes!—plain old BF, as in boyfriend. *Maybe*. I mean, I don't want to be braggy about it, because it's not as if he rented a billboard and painted "I LOVE WINNIE" across it for all the world to see. And please, we are *not* to the love stage. Nonie, nonie, no.

But he did hold my hand, tee hee. He held my hand for the first and only time last Thursday, and it was glorious. Plus he's absolutely gorgeous, with his hazel eyes and slouchy-boy saunter and messy, adorable hair. He jokes around with me, and sometimes I feel almost normal with him, and I definitely have the thought that I could be even more normal around him one day, with practice and mental pep talks and *shoulders back, stomach in* reminders. And then, far off in the future, we can get married and watch TV together and have billions of little Larses and Winnies.

No! Ack! Where did *that* come from?

Please don't let Lars have received that as a weird psychic message through the stratosphere, I begged the world. Sometimes, even though I knew it was impossible, I feared my innermost thoughts *could* be heard. Not just by God, but by unintended recipients like my dead grandfather and a certain hazel-eyed boy.

Just kidding! I thought loudly. *Not planning on marriage, at least not for a long, long time! Not that desperate and girly!*

It did unnerve me, liking Lars and having him (yes, just admit it) like me back. That was a big part of why I had so much to be thankful for, on this day of becoming a teenager. And when I said that a thirteen-year-old should have the world as her oyster, what I meant was this: I hope my life will be this good forever. I hope my life will always be a secret pearl, shimmery and full of promise.

Thirteen-year-olds are too old to blow out candles (though I know I will anyway), but that's my birthday wish.

Dinah's dad pulled into our driveway at five, and Cinnamon's dad followed right on his heels. Or wheels, rather. Dinah and Cinnamon both live with their dads: Dinah because her mom died way back when she was a baby, and Cinnamon because her parents are divorced. Her mom lives in North Carolina, a three-hour drive from Atlanta. Cinnamon has a stepmom, but it isn't a great thing. Her stepmom puts people down a lot, including Cinnamon.

Cinnamon's dad is cool, though. He's a hotshot Atlanta developer who has big-time clients, and sometimes he gets us tickets to random concerts.

Cinnamon hopped out of her father's Lexus and ran up the driveway, past Dinah who was still saying "bye" to her dad. I bounced on my toes on the front porch.

"Happy birthday, you birthday-having fool!" Cinnamon cried, giving me a big ol' hug.

I grinned. "Thanks."

Dinah kissed her dad's cheek in the front seat of their station wagon. They were very close, in a totally sweet way, and I was glad for both of them, because I think you'd need that if someone you love died. She climbed out, got her overnight bag from the backseat, and came to join us. She and Cinnamon were going to spend the night even though it was a Sunday—so cool! We squealed and did a group-hug-spazzy-thing. We were like jumping elephants.

"Party time!" Cinnamon said.

I helped the two of them lug their stuff inside, then called out to Mom.

"We're ready!" I said. "It's time to go! Our personal beautician awaits!"

"Not beautician," Cinnamon said. "Beauticians are frumpy old ladies who went to beauty school."

"With big hair," Dinah contributed.

"Our personal makeup consultant awaits," Cinnamon said.

"*Riiight*," I said, like *thank you, O Wise One*.

Mom clopped downstairs in her heels and a snazzy pants-and-blouse combo. She wore such *Mom* clothes, tailored and put-together. Even when she wore jeans, they were crisp and dark blue and high-waisted, with her shirts tucked in according to the law for forty-year-olds. She was cute in her little outfits.

"Hi, girls," she said.

"Hi, Mrs. Perry," Dinah and Cinnamon chorused.

"So let's do it," she said, because she still thought she was hip. To Dad—who showed up in the kitchen to see us off—she said, "See you on the flip side, homie."

"Oh dear god," I said, as Dinah and Cinnamon giggled. "Mom? Do not *ever* say that again."

Mom laughed. "Tell me not to say something, and that's exactly what I'll greet you with the next time I pick you up from school. *And* I'll be wearing clown shoes."

"Have fun, girls," Dad said, ruffling my hair and then Dinah's and then Cinnamon's. "Just don't go too crazy!"

• • •

At Lenox, Mom told the woman behind the Bobbi Brown counter at Neiman Marcus that we were "only" thirteen (which wasn't even true, Dinah was still twelve) and to please give us a look that was "appropriate." Then she gave me her credit card, said we could all pick one product to buy, and went off to check out the sales rack in the women's department.

"Okay, this is going to be fun," the Bobbi Brown lady said as soon as Mom was out of earshot. She was Asian, with gorgeous pale skin and dark eye makeup. I guessed she was in her late twenties. "My name's Aimee, and I say let's just go for it. What do you think?"

"I think I like Aimee very much," Cinnamon said under her breath.

"Winnie first, because she's the birthday girl," Dinah said.

"No, I want to go last," I said. I was excited about being made over, because I myself was crappy with makeup, and so pretty much avoided it like the plague. And it seemed so naked and embarrassing to have it on your face, visible to the world in a way that said, "Hey, look! I care about being pretty!"

Except I *do* care about being pretty. *Der*. I don't think there's a single person in the world who doesn't care about being pretty. Any female, at any rate.

Well . . . backtrack, backtrack, backtrack. I *used* to not care what I looked like. On a scale of one to ten, my appearance scored about a "two" in terms of importance. One more weirdness of getting older: appearance now ranks way higher, like even an eight or nine.

But I didn't want to be the first to get made over, because I'd been struck with a sudden case of the jitters. The naked thing again.

"Do me," Cinnamon said. She hiked herself onto the stool. "I want smoldering, baby." She growled. "I am a tigress!"

"You got it," Aimee said.

She smoothed moisturizer over Cinnamon's skin to provide "a good base" and explained that Cinnamon didn't need foundation. "None of you girls do," she said. "Enjoy it while you can."

She stroked green eye shadow over Cinnamon's lids, which she said Cinnamon could pull off because of her green eyes, and used a black eyeliner around her eyes. "But only from the middle of the iris out," she said. "You don't want your eyes looking squinched together."

Cinnamon blinked at Aimee's touch, although she was clearly trying to hold still. The eyeliner made Cinnamon's eyes "pop," to use Aimee's expression.

She finished the look with jet black mascara and something called a "color brick" on Cinnamon's cheeks. It was a cool shimmery blush that was a mix of three different pinks.

"Ta-da," she said, twirling the stool so that Cinnamon faced us like a painting.

Dinah drew in her breath. "You are so gorgeous!" she said.

"Yeah?" Cinnamon said.

"You look terrific," I said. She did, in a striking, daring, club-girl way that was perfect for her. It was a look I could never pull off. It just wasn't me. "You look so old!"

Cinnamon hopped off the stool and picked up a hand-held mirror. "Aw, man, I *love* it," she told Aimee. "And I already know I want that color brick thing for sure. Or maybe the eye shadow!"

"Would you wear the eye shadow to school?" I asked.

"Yes," Cinnamon said, like, *Of course, why wouldn't I?*

"Your turn," Aimee said to Dinah. She patted the stool. "Hop on up here, sweetie."

That made Cinnamon and me laugh. *Sweetie.*

Dinah blushed. Out of all of us, she had the absolute least experience with makeup, because of having no mom or stepmom or older sisters. And because, even though she was twelve, she didn't always act it. When it came to makeup and boys and stuff like that, she acted more eleven-ish, or maybe even ten.

Like how she was wiggling backward onto the stool, adjusting her bottom by lifting up one cheek and then the other. When it was my turn, I'd do a quick, confident hop, like Cinnamon had. I wouldn't adjust my bottom.

"Let's see," Aimee said, tilting her head to study Dinah's features. Dinah held her smile in a way that showed she knew she was being scrutinized. Round face, white skin, blue eyes—that was Dinah. My little kitty-cat girl, *so* not a tigress. Which was as it should be. In a threesome of friends, there isn't room for more than one tigress.

Aimee got to work with something called "Moon Glow," which she said would "add radiance" to Dinah's skin. "It has reflective particles that catch the light and bounce it back," she explained. "Angelina Jolie uses it."

Dinah giggled. She jutted her chin forward to meet Aimee's touch.

Aimee stroked on a smoky eye shadow and lightly lined Dinah's blue eyes with gray eyeliner. I noted how she did it, with lots of small dashes rather than one continuous line. She used a tiny brush to paint Dinah's lips with a deep cherry stain.

"There," she said. "What do you think?"

Dinah looked in the mirror. Cinnamon and I leaned over her shoulders.

"Whoa," Cinnamon said when she got her words back. As for me, I remained speechless. Dinah looked . . . beautiful. How had Aimee done that? Was it the cherry-red lips? Or maybe it was the Moon Glow. Dinah's skin was luminescent.

"Oh my gosh," Dinah said. She put down the mirror and grabbed a Kleenex, rubbing at her lips.

"What are you doing? Leave it!" Cinnamon said.

"It's too red!" Dinah said. "I look like a . . . like a streetwalker!"

Aimee laughed. "Sweetie, you do *not* look like a streetwalker."

She kept scrubbing. "I do!"

"Dinah, stop," Cinnamon said. She grabbed Dinah's hand. "You're not used to it, that's all."

I wasn't used to it, either. I was confused by what I was feeling, which I recognized by its prickly claws in my stomach.

"Honest, you look fabulous," I said, trying to push the jealousy away. Jealousy was stupid and wrong, especially when it came to Dinah. I should be happy she looked so great! I was happy. I *was*.

"Anyway, it's just for fun," I said. "Nobody says you have to make yourself up every day."

"You've got to get that lip stain," Cinnamon said. "That has to be your one thing."

"Well, don't *force* her." I laughed. "Dinah, it's totally up to you."

She got off the stool, easing herself down until her feet touched the floor. It was downright weird seeing this beautiful Dinah. I couldn't get over it.

Aimee patted the stool to say it was my turn, while Dinah gravitated to one of the mirrors on the counter.

I tore my eyes away. I hopped up on the stool and straightened my spine. Then I felt stupid and let myself slump. Then I felt slumpy and straightened up again. Ack! Why was I was so awkward in my body?!

"Hold still," Aimee said. She did her thing with the

moisturizer, her fingers light and birdlike, and I focused on soaking into the moment. *This is your birthday treat, and you're supposed to enjoy it*, I reminded myself. It was part of my normal existence to give myself instructions like this. Maybe other people acted and lived in total naturalness. I often wondered if they did. But me? I needed an operating manual.

"For you, we'll go with dark brown eyeliner," Aimee said. "You have such pretty eyes. We want to emphasize that."

That made me feel better. *Pretty eyes, I have pretty eyes.* Were Dinah and Cinnamon catching this? No, Dinah was still peering at her at reflection and Cinnamon was uncapping lipsticks and testing them on her forearm. I felt a stab of irritation. I'd watched them get made over. Shouldn't they be watching me?

Cinnamon felt my gaze and glanced up. "Looking good!" she encouraged.

Aimee applied a pink glitter dust called "Rock Star" to my eyelids, and she used a miniature comb to smooth my eyebrows. "You'll probably want to pluck eventually," she said, "but let's not worry about that now."

What was that supposed to mean? Am I a hairy, over-eyebrowed beast? Or—oh god. Maybe I had a monobrow?

"Do I have a monobrow?" I asked.

"Not at all," Aimee said. "Everyone can benefit from a little shaping, that's all."

"Oh," I said. But what I thought was: *Then why didn't you mention it to Cinnamon and Dinah? Couldn't they benefit from a little shaping, too?*

I really, really hated how needy I was feeling. It was as if it came out of nowhere.

"Um . . . should we use the Moon Glow?" I asked.

"Not with your skin tone," Aimee said.

I wanted to argue, but didn't.

She reached into a drawer and pulled out a steel something-or-other that looked like it came from the Middle Ages. It was curved at the end, with a black cushiony pad between two parts that opened and shut. Aimee put her hand under my chin and said, "Okay, look down for me."

I did. She clamped my eyelashes and squeezed. *Ah*, I thought. *An eyelash curler*. It didn't hurt. She did the other eye, then stroked brown mascara on both with a fat brush. She finished up with a pale pink lip gloss.

"There," she said.

Dinah and Cinnamon stopped doing their own stuff and gathered around.

"Oh, *Winnie*," Dinah said.

"Sheesh, girl," Cinnamon said. "You're a babe!"

I looked at myself in the mirror. My eyelashes, which I'd never spent much time thinking about, curled in a dark fringe around my eyes. The pink glitter dust didn't look awful, as I'd feared. It made my eyes sparkly. And the gloss—again, pink—made my lips shiny and soft.

I'd never thought of myself as a pink kind of girl. . . . but maybe I was.

"You like?" Aimee asked.

I nodded. I *did* like, very much.

Cinnamon and Dinah put their faces down by mine so that all of us were visible in the mirror. We were ourselves, only fancier. The heaviness in my chest lifted and floated away, all but the teeniest tendril.

"Three beauties," Aimee pronounced.

"Aren't we, though?" Cinnamon said. "We are *foxy*."

Dinah and I giggled. I was filled with love for both of them, and I felt guilty for not always being *only* filled with love. When it came time to pick out which product we each wanted to buy, I told Dinah she really should get the lip stain.

"It makes you look fifteen at least," I say.

"Oh," she said. Then, "Do I want to look fifteen?"

I hesitated. Didn't she? Didn't we all?

"Of course," Cinnamon said. She turned to me and tut-tutted. "Kids. What can you do?"

"Oh, please," Dinah said. "Like you're *so* much older."

"Eons and eons, *sweetie*," Cinnamon threw back.

I smiled, but I wondered who was right: Cinnamon for wanting to move forward, or Dinah for wanting to stay put? And where did I fit in?

"Get the lip stain," I said decisively. "And I'll buy the Rock Star glitter dust."

"But—" Dinah started.

"Nope, no arguing. And Cinnamon, you should get the color brick, because you can get green eye shadow anywhere."

"Not this exact shade," she protested.

"Fine, get the eye shadow," I said.

"Okay," she said happily.

Dinah said the Bobbi Brown products were the best birthday favors ever, and I teased her for calling them "favors," as if I was five again and handing out cellophane bags filled with candy and those cheapo soundmakers that unfurl when you blow them.

At the photo booth by the food court, we posed for three different strips of pictures, some goofy and some for real. Later that night, when we were back at my house, we cut the strips apart and divvied up the pics. I picked one, then Cinnamon, then Dinah. Then all over again until every photo was claimed.

"You have *got* to give that one to Lars," Cinnamon said of one in particular. In it, I was laughing, and my hair was swished back in a particularly flattering way. My eyes were bright and happy.

"I don't think so," I said. We were in my bedroom, all three of us sprawled on our stomachs on the carpet. The pictures were spread in front of us.

"Why not?" she said.

"Because it would be too obvious, that's why. What,

I'm just going to whip it out and say, 'Here, this is for you'?"

"Uh . . . yes."

"Uh . . . *no.*" I glanced at Dinah for support. She tittered.

"Don't you want him to see how hot you are?" Cinnamon said.

"Not if I have to be the one who shows him!"

"Then I'll do it," she said, deftly exchanging my swished-hair picture for one from her own collection.

"Hey!" I protested.

"Yeah, whatever," Cinnamon said. She stacked her pics and slipped them into her back pocket, where I couldn't grab them without being a perv.

My cheeks got hot, because she knew and I knew and even Dinah knew that I *did* want Lars to see. Just as long as Cinnamon was subtle about it. . . . which, given the fact that she was Cinnamon, was totally a crapshoot.

But making a big deal out of it would only egg her on. I picked up the photo she'd given me in exchange for the one of me as a babe. It was one of the goofy ones, with Cinnamon mugging for the camera and Dinah stretching her mouth out with her fingers. I lurched at an angle behind them, making a deranged, hairy-eyeball face.

I imagined Cinnamon giving Lars this one and snort-giggled.

"What?" Cinnamon said.

"Nothing," I said.

"Seriously. *What?*" Cinnamon hated being left out of a joke.

I shrugged. No way was I planting the idea in her head. It did make me realize, though, how thankful I should be that we *had* traded. It was a nugget of unexpected good.

"Just . . . you know," I said. "Thinking about oysters."

"*Oysters*?" Cinnamon repeated.

Dinah abruptly sat up. "Winnie, please tell me you don't have an oyster hidden somewhere."

"What are you *talking* about?" Cinnamon demanded. "Did anyone bring up oysters? No, I don't think so. Oysters are not a part of this conversation!"

I laughed.

"Oysters, be gone!" she cried.

"Tell me right now there are no oysters lurking about," Dinah said. "I mean it."

"No oysters, I promise. Only symbolic oysters."

"*Symbolic* oysters?" Cinnamon said.

"Yep," I said grandly. I rolled onto my back and gazed at the ceiling. "And in every symbolic oyster is a symbolic pearl."

Cinnamon groaned, which only added to my pleasure. The carpet was nubbly against my skin, and I realized that the lingering sadness I'd felt at the mall was no longer present. Instead I felt expansive and happy.

Yes, there is both good and bad in the world, and more often than not, they're mixed together. At least, that's how it seems to me. But it's the oyster thing again, because maybe the trick is to find the good part and pull it out and say, "There! See?"

I could do that. I could do anything.

I was thirteen.

April

I WANTED LARS. I did. I *wanted* him. Not in a hot-and-heavy "let's make out" sort of way, because that was not within the realm of possibility at this juncture of my life. ("Juncture." I loved it. I loved finding words like that and tossing them about, even if just in my own mind. "Flotsam and jetsam." "Indubitably." "Segue," with that lovely "*way*" sound at the end, despite the deceptive spelling.)

No, I didn't want to make out with Lars—yet. I just wanted to own him, to have him be mine. I wanted him the way I wanted a new bike when I was younger, or the Easy-Bake Oven.

I kept waiting for something to happen between us, for us to at least hold hands again, but somehow the world had yet to throw us into that perfect situation where hand-holding would be the only possible response.

It made me feel desperate, how much I ached for him. I'd have daydreams about him, stupid stuff like him finding me at my locker and putting his hands over my eyes, then leaning close and murmuring "Hey there" into my ear. Or—and this one was kind of embarrassing—I had this one fantasy that I'd fall asleep on one of the benches out on the quad (because I did sometimes curl up on them for a quickie little snooze), and he'd find me and think how cute I looked. Or not *cute*, but pretty. And maybe I'd be wearing a miniskirt, and I wouldn't be indecent or anything, but he'd notice that I had nice legs. He'd say, "Wake up, sleepyhead," and I would. I'd be all flustered and drowsy-eyed, and he'd grin like he found me so incredibly charming.

My daydreams made me feel lame, though, because I was sure he didn't think about me as much as I thought about him. Well, fairly sure. I hoped he did, but I also knew that boys were different creatures than girls, as evidenced by my dear, sweet, nutty brother, Ty. I loved him with all my heart, but I worried about him sometimes.

Like now, for instance. The sound of duct tape being ripped from the roll jerked me out of my Lars fantasies and dropped me back into cold, hard reality.

"Ty, what are you doing?" I asked. It was Monday morning. We'd leave for school in five minutes. Mom would drop Ty off at Trinity, while I'd ride with Sandra to Westminster.

"Taping up my pants," Ty said. He ripped a foot-long strip of Day-Glo orange from the roll. He wrapped it around the leg of his gray sweats, affixing it to his ankle.

"Okay, yeah. Got that," I said. "*Why?*"

"So snakes can't crawl in," he said. He frowned. The tape was misbehaving and getting all twisty at the end.

"Ty," I said, "there are no snakes at Trinity."

"How do you know? How do you know *for sure*?" he asked. "You never know. That's what you told me last night."

Well, true. But that was because I was in charge of making him take his bath, and he had refused to wash his hair. Should a six-year-old refuse to wash his hair? No. Should a six-year-old need bath-time supervision at all? No again. Ty was such the baby of the family. One of these days he was going to have to grow up, and then what was he going to do?

But yes. I'd played the lice card, telling him that lice loved dirty scalps and you never knew when a louse was on the prowl.

It worked, and now I was paying the price.

"I wasn't talking about snakes," I said.

"If a rattlesnake crawls in my pants, it will bite me," Ty said. He ripped and pasted one last strip. "Now it can't, because I have foiled it. Ha ha!"

He straightened up. His sweats bagged around his skinny legs, then tapered at his shins, bound messily with orange tape. He was Duct-Tape-Boy, with his hair all stick-y-up-y from falling asleep with it wet.

"Don't you think people will . . ."

"What?"

Laugh at you, I'd been about to say. But it seemed cruel. Ty was six. He shouldn't have to deal with the harshness of fashion.

Then again, maybe it would be crueler to let him march off like that?

I came at it more gently. "Do other kids tape their pants up?"

"No," he said. He thought for a moment. "But Lexie has sparkly pants."

"She does?"

His lips twitched in a way that was new for him this year—which I guess showed that he was growing up more than I gave him credit for. It was a twitch that meant *I want to tell you this, but I'm also self-conscious. A little. But not so much that I'm not going to tell you anyway.* "I like her in her sparkly pants."

"Uh-*huh*."

"That's why I'm taping my pants. That *and* the snakes." Again the mouth-twitch, along with a glance to make sure I wouldn't make fun of him. "I want to be brave for Lexie."

"And taping up your pants makes you brave?"

"Yes," he said, "because if I am brave in my heart, knowing that snakes can't get in, then I will be brave on the outside, too."

"Ahhh," I said. Well, it made a goofy sort of sense, I guess. I just hoped Lexie went for boys with duct-taped sweats.

Mom hurried in. She was running late, as usual. "Come on, Ty, let's go," she said. She took in Ty's pants. A pained look crossed her face, which then de-wrinkled into a resigned *oh well* expression.

"Last week a little boy named Daniel wore a pirate costume," she told me.

"And he peed on the playground," Ty added. "He did a tree-pee, which is not allowed."

"A first-grader peed on the playground?" I said.

"He did it so the teachers couldn't see," Ty said.

Mom narrowed her eyes. "Ty, you are *not* to pee on the playground."

"Mom!" he protested. "I would never!"

"Just like you would never pick your nose?"

"I don't! I quit!"

"I certainly hope so." She swooped up her purse from the granite counter. "Okay, we're off. Winnie, tell Sandra she better get a move on."

"Sandra!" I bellowed, arching my head toward the living room, which led by way of traveling air molecules to Sandra's upstairs bedroom. "Get a move on!"

Mom's look said, *Gee, Winnie, thanks*, but she didn't bother to scold me. She strode out the back door, and Ty scurried after her.

Several minutes later, Sandra thundered downstairs, her hair flying and her Chuck Taylors unlaced. She didn't take the time to grab a package of Pop-Tarts. She didn't even glance at me. "Let's go," is all she said.

Uh-oh, I thought. *Bad mood*.

In the front seat of her rattly old BMW, which she'd saved up for herself last year, I waited for her to spill. She didn't.

"What's wrong?" I finally asked.

"Nothing," she said.

I gazed out the window. Sandra's cell phone, visible in the pouch of her messenger bag, played a snippet of an old Doors song: "Hello, I love you. Won't you tell me your name?"

"Want me to answer it?" I asked.

"No, I do not."

I fished it out and checked the name. "It's Bo."

She snatched it before I could press the green "talk" button.

"I said *no*," she snapped. "What do you not understand about that?"

I shrank. Sandra was often a grump, but not usually a mean grump. And why wouldn't she want to talk to Bo, whom she'd been going out with for two years? Bo was the most perfect guy in the world. He was captain of the high school baseball team. He was funny and sweet and had muscles, but not in a cheesy way. He loved doughnuts.

Plus he was nice to Ty and me, and not to impress Sandra. Sometimes he'd show up at our house before Sandra got home, and he'd hang out and watch *Oprah* with us. Or *Ellen*, which was becoming my new favorite. *Not* Dr. Phil. Ty would force Bo to admire the spear he'd made or whatever, and Bo would give him ideas about how to make it better, like soaking a leather shoelace in water and wrapping it around the part where the arrowhead was attached, so that when it dried, it was super tight and looked all authentic.

I loved Bo. I was probably a little *in* love with Bo, even though I was also intensely in like with Lars.

"Are you guys having a fight?" I asked Sandra.

"No," she said.

Then why don't you want to talk to him? I wanted to say. But I didn't, because the energy she was radiating told me I'd only get barked at. I was very much a wimp when it came to conflict. Anyone's conflict. Cinnamon would tell me about these knockdown, drag-out screaming matches she had with her dad, over stupid stuff like her cell minutes or how much time she spent on the Internet, and part of me would be in awe. At the same time, just hearing her stories made my stomach get tight.

Sandra's phone stopped ringing. A few seconds later, it did its voice mail bleep.

"Do you want me to check it for you?" I asked timidly.

"No. And I don't want you asking about it. I don't want you talking at all." She glared at me. "Do you think you can do that?"

She said it like I was a baby, like, *Do you think that's remotely possible? Do you think, maybe, you can get that through your head?*

It stung. I had my own boy problems, not that she'd ever asked. And Ty was the baby, not me. Although even Ty had girl problems, apparently.

We rode the rest of the way in silence. She dropped me off at the junior high building, and I got out without looking at her.

"Bye," she said grudgingly. There might have been a smidgen of apology in it.

Whatever, I thought. But because I was me, I muttered "bye" back. I didn't even slam the door.

Over lunch, I vented to Dinah and Cinnamon. Dinah slurped her chocolate milk, nodding with wide eyes, while Cinnamon scowled on my behalf. She shoved around her carrot sticks, which she was eating to try and lose weight. That made her scowly, too.

"She turned the whole day bad," I complained. "She took her own stupid mood and forced it on me."

"Do you think she and Bo are going to break up?" Dinah asked.

"They better not," Cinnamon said. She and Dinah were Bo fans, too. "She'd be throwing away the best thing that ever happened to her."

"I know," I said.

"She doesn't deserve him," Cinnamon went on. "He's, like, a golden boy. She's a pile of poop."

"Well . . . not a pile of *poop*," I said.

"Sandra's really nice when she's not being a jerk," Dinah said loyally. "She could be a golden girl if she wanted. If she were a cheerleader."

"Sandra would never be a cheerleader," I said. "She's more like the anti-cheerleader."

"Except she's still really beautiful," Dinah said.

Cinnamon admitted it with a nod. I felt a familiar pang, because I knew I wasn't.

I changed the subject. Kind of. "It's like, everything

comes back to boy-girl stuff. Sandra's fighting with Bo. Ty's in a tizzy over this girl, Lexie, and you want to know why? Because her pants are sparkly."

Cinnamon snorted.

"And Lars hardly ever talks to me except in class, and then it's just to say *comment ça va* and *où se trouve la bibliotheque*!" Even though Lars was in eighth grade and I was in seventh, we had French together.

"At least he doesn't take Spanish," Cinnamon said. Cinnamon took Spanish. Señor Torres made the girls partner up with girls and the boys partner up with boys, because of hormones.

"It's so annoying, though!" I said. "He did hold my hand, right? I didn't make that up, did I?"

"He did," Dinah said. "I saw."

"There was definite hand-to-hand contact," Cinnamon agreed.

It had happened publicly, the hand-holding, which at the time made it all the more miraculous. Lars and I were outside the junior high building waiting to be picked up, and his hand reached over and grabbed mine. *His* grabbed *mine*. *He* initiated.

Should a guy hold a girl's hand if he's never going to do it again?

No, he should not.

"Listen, Win," Cinnamon said.

I looked at her, wishing she wouldn't call me "Win."

"Win" was Lars's name for me, just as "Lars" was my name for him. His real name was "Larson," which was nice, but "Lars" was better.

"When it comes to love, you have to be fierce," she said. "Sometimes the girl has to make the move. Sad, but true."

I sighed. "I *am* fierce in love. You cannot call me un-fierce in love. Right, Dinah?"

"Huh?" She grabbed one of my fries, which I was too heartsick to eat anyway.

"With Toby," I said. "Remember?"

"Oh, god," Cinnamon said. "The guy who was your sixth grade Valentine's Day crush? Please tell me we're not going back to that."

"You weren't there, so shush," I said. Cinnamon was an alpha-omega at Westminster, meaning that she'd been here since Pre-K. Dinah and I had gone to Trinity through sixth, and then switched over. Toby, on the other hand, now went to Woodward.

"Winnie was very brave with Toby," Dinah affirmed. "She called him up and pledged her undying affection."

I blushed. "*No.*"

"And his brother made fun of her, and it was very scarring," Dinah went on.

"Which is my point exactly," I said. "Being fierce in love isn't always the best solution!"

"Dude," Cinnamon warned, her expression shifting.

It was unnecessary. My super-ultra-sensitive Lars radar

had kicked in the very same second, noting even before Cinnamon did that he was strolling into the cafeteria. I turned into hyper-Winnie, putting on a show.

"*Di*nah!" I exclaimed, slapping her hand as it snaked for another fry. "Leave some for me, will you?" I laughed stupidly and loudly, monitoring Lars's progress from the corners of my eyes.

"You're a freak," Cinnamon said. "You know that, don't you?"

"Silly Cinnamon!" I said, smiling as if I were a Miss Universe contestant. Was Lars watching? Did he see me?

"He's coming *ov*-er," Dinah said.

My heart went bambitty-bam. "Teeth?" I said, baring my lips.

"They're fine," Dinah said.

"Except for the wad of spinach," Cinnamon contributed.

"Do you see any spinach on my plate?" I asked. Anything to keep talking—this was not the time to be unanimated. "No, you do not."

"Then it must have been from dinner last night," she replied.

"I think it's time for you to be quiet," I sang. I turned around, glowing (hopefully) with wittiness and joie de vivre. "Oh! Lars! Hi!"

He was behind me, his hands jammed in his pockets. "Hey, Win," he said. He jerked his chin at my friends. "Hey, Cinnamon. Dinah."

"Hey, Lars," Cinnamon said. "What's kickin'?"

What's kickin'—she cracked me up. Only I was too jittery to enjoy it. This was what happened when a boy held your hand and then inexplicably never did again. You started to doubt yourself. You stopped finding the humor in everyday life. Curse false-hand-holding boys!

Except not really. I wanted to touch him, not curse him.

"Not much," Lars said. He focused on me. "You finish the French assignment?"

"*J'aime le hotdog*," I said in reply. I cleverly translated it for the others. "That means 'I like the hot dog.'"

"I bet you do," Cinnamon said under her breath.

I drove my sneaker into her shin. "Our assignment was to pretend we were at a sporting event? Okay?"

"She uptalks when she's nervous," Cinnamon said to Lars. He chuckled, but her comment made me mad. And embarrassed.

"I'm not *nervous*," I said.

"I like hot dogs," Dinah offered. When we all looked at her, she said, "What? I do!"

"*Thank* you," I said. I wasn't sure for what; maybe just for being Dinah. For being . . . without guile. Sometimes, with Cinnamon, it was like she fell into this "impress the guy" mode and forgot the primary rule of friendship, which was to make your bud look good in front of her boy. Not stupid.

"So," Lars said. "See you in class?"

I rose above my embarrassment and put on my game face: flirty, but casual. Or at least the illusion of casual. I hoped.

"If you're lucky," I said.

"Ooo!" Cinnamon crowed.

Lars's mouth did an adorable sideways quirk-thing. "Oh, is *that* how it is?"

"Uh-huh." There was that fun, amped-up charge between us, and I willed him to take that energy and run with it. *Tousle my hair*, I commanded him telepathically. *You're standing right there. Do it!*

"Well, here's hoping I get lucky," he said.

Cinnamon hooted again, and I was aware of Dinah giggling. I grinned up at Lars, and he grinned back. It was nice.

But I wanted more.

On Tuesday, Ty asked me what he could do to make Lexie like him. I said, "I don't know, ask Sandra." Then I remembered that she and Bo were having their little tiff or whatever. "On the other hand, don't."

"But what should I do?" Ty asked.

"Well, let's think about it," I said. We were in the backyard, squished together in the hammock. Ty was warm and little-kid sweaty against me. "On the playground, when y'all have break, what does Lexie like to do?"

"She and Claire chase boys and try to kiss them," he said.

"Does she chase you?"

"No."

"Why not?"

"I don't know. Do *you* know?"

"Hmm," I said. I loved that he thought I might, but it was a burden, too. Sometimes it was as if he saw me as God, when I was *so* not. "When Lexie and Claire are doing that, what do you do?"

"Nothing."

"You just sit there like a lump?"

"I walk around the edge of the playground. And I look at things."

"Like what?"

"Lexie."

My brother, the stalker. Lovely.

"Sometimes I tell her to fall down," he went on, "but only when she can't hear me."

"What? Why would you do that?"

"If she hurt her knee, I could take her to the office," he said. "I could take her to get a Band-Aid."

It made my heart ache, this honesty of his. And the sweetness of wanting to take Lexie to get a Band-Aid. I imagined him standing on the fringes, orange duct tape radiating from his pants cuffs, and, like me, just wanting something *more*.

"If I were in first grade, I would totally chase you," I told him.

"And try to kiss me? On the lips?"

"Do Lexie and Claire kiss the boys on the *lips*?" I said incredulously.

He shrugged. "Maybe."

Whoa. If so, they'd gone further than I had. How pathetic was that?

"Let's just swing," I said. I nudged the grass to make the hammock sway.

"Okay. We can be baby spiders, and we can't touch the ground or the birds will get us."

"Uh-huh."

"And you are my big sister bird. I mean spider. *Reek! Reek!*"

Is that what baby spiders said? *Reek reek?*

He said it again, in distress.

"It's all right, baby spider," I said, pulling him close. "I'm here."

On Friday morning, I woke up early so that I could get in and out of the shower by seven. Today was Sandra's seventeenth birthday (twenty-six days after mine), and this was my present to her. This way Sandra could take a super long shower and not be rushed. I'd also made her a pair of earrings, but I'd give them to her later.

Over breakfast—which Sandra actually had time to sit down and eat, thanks to me—I asked her what her birthday plans were. She said she didn't know, that she'd probably do something with Elizabeth and Raelynn. Which I thought was wrong. Why wasn't she spending it with Bo?

"You don't think friends are as important as a boyfriend?" she said when I asked.

"Well, sure, but—"

"That is so lame," she said. "You would make the worst feminist."

"That's not true!" I said. "I'm totally a feminist. I'm a great feminist!"

"*Pfff*," Sandra said, and not entirely without reason. I wasn't actually sure I *was* a feminist. Truth be told, I wasn't exactly sure what being a feminist meant, other than sometimes they didn't shave their legs, and, yeah, um, that wasn't going to happen.

"But what about Bo?" I asked.

"What about him?"

"Are you guys still fighting?"

"When were we fighting? What makes you think we're fighting?"

"Because . . ." I didn't like putting it in words. "That day, you didn't answer when he called."

"I didn't answer one phone call. Big deal. I was annoyed with him."

"Why?"

"It was stupid. I was totally being stupid," she said. "On Sunday he went to this girl Kristi's house to study, and I guess I got jealous."

"You did?" I said. She'd given me an unexpected peek into her life as a junior, where boyfriends went over to other girls' houses to study, and I wanted to know more. I was especially curious about Kristi. Was she cute? Did she have a thing for Bo? Was she trying to steal him away?

"But I got over it," Sandra said.

"Did Bo?" I asked.

"*Yes*. Of *course*. Why would you even say that?"

"Well, because it's your birthday. It just seems weird that he . . . I mean, not *bad* weird, necessarily, just—"

"He has plans," she said shortly. She blinked back a sudden rush of tears, which was completely un-Sandra-like. She chomped off a bite of bagel, chewed ferociously, and wouldn't meet my eyes.

Oh. This wasn't her choice. A lump rose in my throat.

"Winnie!" Mom called from the stairs. "Could you come here, please?"

"Um, sure." I shoved back my chair, glad for an excuse to leave.

"I need you to talk to Ty," Mom said. She was standing outside the kids' bathroom. From within, I could hear Ty crying. "He's being ridiculous."

"I am *not*!" Ty yelled. "I want them back! I *need* them!"

"Ty," Mom said.

"They were"—big snotty sniffle—"my *friends*!"

"What is he talking about?" I asked.

"His fingernails," Mom said wearily. She looked at me like, *Do you understand now why I feel like pulling my hair out?* "They needed to be clipped. I asked him if he wanted me to do it. He said 'yes.'"

"I changed my mind!" Ty cried from behind the door.

Well, neither one of them were getting anywhere this way.

"No, but—"

"Did *he* call *you* his archenemy?"

"No, but—"

"Did you chase after him and try to kiss him?"

"No!" I grabbed his bony shoulders and shook him. "You are a crazy boy! Shut your mouth, you crazy thing!"

He giggled, which was a good sign. "Girls and boys kiss when they like each other," he said. "*Tongue*-kiss."

"Where did you hear about tongue kissing?" I demanded.

"I don't know. But I bet Sandra will tongue-kiss Bo when she finds out about the surprise party."

"Surprise party? What surprise party?"

He clapped his hand over his mouth. Through his fingers, he said, "Oops. I'm not supposed to tell."

"You can tell me," I said. "Is Bo throwing Sandra a surprise party?"

"He came over yesterday. I had to go up to Sandra's room and get one of her rings, so he could see what size it was. And then he gave it back. He's going to give her a whole new one tonight, when he surprises her."

Excitement bubbled up in my veins. Bo wasn't secretly dumping Sandra for Kristi! He was throwing her a surprise party, she just didn't know it! *And* he was giving her a ring, which was very symbolic, even if it wasn't—of course—an actual engagement ring.

I was so happy for Sandra. It made me buzz.

"Listen," I said to Ty. "Maybe today you could ask Lexie

to do something, like go swing, and then she'd know she wasn't your archenemy."

"Any*more*," Ty said.

"Right. Although she never really was."

Ty thought about this. I let him.

"If I do that with Lexie, will you do it, too?" he asked at last.

"What do you mean?"

"With the boy *you* like."

My heart fluttered, jacking up the adrenaline already flowing through me. "In junior high, people don't swing."

"Why not?"

"We don't even have a swing set!"

"Oh." He tilted his head. "Then will you kiss him? On the lips?"

"Ty! *No*!"

"Then I'm not asking Lexie to swing."

I gaped at him. He was *good*.

I regained my composure. I couldn't let a six-year-old get the best of me.

"Dude," I said, feeling like Cinnamon. "I will *maybe* kiss him, *if* I ever get the chance."

Ty grinned.

"*If*," I said again, holding up a finger to stress the conditional nature of my promise.

"Okay," he said. He nudged the trash can between his legs. "Now will you tape my fingernails back on?"

"No, but I'll put them in a baggie for you."

"And I can keep them? Forever?"

"And you can keep them forever."

He scrambled off the tub. "I'll go get the bag."

He ran out of the bathroom. A few seconds later, Mom came in.

"Thank you, Winnie," she said.

"No problem," I said. I paused. "It wasn't the fingernails. It was something else."

"It always is," Mom said.

"A girl."

"Great."

But she didn't sound all that alarmed, and I had a horrible thought. "You weren't listening, were you? Outside the door?"

She assured me she hadn't, and my panic smoothed out. *Whew*.

I did kind of want to touch base with her about it, though. Not the Lars part or the tongue kissing, just the boy-girl thing in general.

"It's odd that it starts so young," I said. "Don't you think?"

"It's the way of humans," Mom said. "You, for example, were a flirt from the moment you were born."

"Oh, please."

"When you were a baby and you saw a handsome man, you'd wink at him."

"*Mom*!"

"Never at the women, just the men. And you'd bat your eyelashes."

I blushed. "Mom, I would not."

"I always worried they'd think I taught you to do that, that I was some desperate housewife using my baby to lure them in." She smiled. "But you did it all on your own. Knowing how to flirt was just . . . wired into you."

"Well, if it was, it's gone now," I said.

"Don't worry, you'll find it again," Mom said.

"I will?"

"I'm absolutely positive. Just . . . not right away, all right?"

Ty reappeared with a Ziploc bag clutched in his hand.

"Here," he said, thrusting it at me.

Mom shook her head and laughed, and I knew what she was thinking. I'd gone from flirt to fingernail-gatherer, and she was glad.

But her tales of me as the Amazing Winking Baby gave me hope, and what *I* was thinking was that what Mom didn't know wouldn't hurt her. And as I plucked little fingernail moons out of the trash, my resolve solidified. I'd made a promise to Ty, and I intended to keep it.

GIRLS, I'VE GOT NEWS," Cinnamon said over our three-way call. "Memorial Park? Fifteen minutes?"

I groaned, not out of lack of interest, but because it was nine o'clock Saturday morning and I was in my PJs. I'd planned on staying in my PJs for hours and days and years.

"Why don't you guys come over here?" I said to her and Dinah. "You could bring beignets."

"No," Cinnamon said decisively. "This is no-unwanted-ears sort of news. I'm talking juicy, baby."

"About what?" Dinah asked.

"You'll have to wait and see."

"Is it about Brad's party?" Dinah pushed. Brad was an eighth grader with actual sideburns and a tattoo of a lizard that no one had ever seen. He threw legendary parties with zero parents on the premises. All three of us were fascinated by Brad—in a repulsed sort of way—but Dinah the most. I figured it was because she liked soap operas, and Brad (and his parties) definitely fell into the soap opera category.

"Maybe," Cinnamon said, which meant yes. None of us had gone to Brad's party last night, because we were lowly seventh graders and hadn't been invited. But Cinnamon's neighbor was an eighth grader named Steffie, who held a mid-level position in the eighth grade popularity scene. Steffie *had* gone to the party.

My guess? Steffie had popped over to Cinnamon's this morning to brag, and now Cinnamon was in the envious position of being able to spread the dirt.

"Was Lars there? Did you hear anything about Lars?" I asked.

"La la la," Cinnamon said. "Memorial Park?"

"Fine," I griped.

"And, Winnie?" Cinnamon said just a wee bit too sweetly.

"What?"

"Do bring beignets. An *excellent* idea."

The sun warmed my neck as I biked from Huey's to Memorial Park, a paper bag holding a dozen beignets and a pint of milk gripped between my fingers and the handlebar. The beignets' powdered-sugary smell puffed up as I pedaled. Yummy yum yum.

At the park, the three of us climbed to the top of the rickety metal play structure, which was shaped in the vaguest of ways like a spider. Or maybe an alien, with curved, runged legs. Either way it was a pathetic, pathetic play structure, and it was high time the city replaced it with one of those snazzy castle-themed dealies all made of wood. But when they did, I knew I'd be sad.

"Here you go," I said to Cinnamon, handing her a beignet. "And here *you* go," I said to Dinah, who looked froglike with her legs scrunched high.

"You are a goddess," Cinnamon said.

"Aren't I?" I pulled out my own beignet and placed it on my leg. The milk was trickier. I opened the cardboard carton, considered my options, then wedged it between my feet, which were propped on a metal crossbar.

"So," I said, after taking my first scrumptious bite of beignet. Powdered sugar snowed onto my shirt. "Spill."

"Well," Cinnamon said. "The first thing you need to know is that the party was unchaperoned, just as I suspected."

"No way," Dinah said.

"Way," Cinnamon said. "Steffie said Brad's parents were at some charity event where they had to dress all wacky."

"*Wacky*," I echoed, saying it in an appropriately wacky way. Wacky was one of those words that couldn't be denied.

"The event was at a hotel, and they stayed overnight, which meant Brad had the whole house to himself," Cinnamon said.

Dinah did a shivery kind of thing, but not because it was cold. Her shiver had more to do with the unnerving and too-old concept of having a party your parents didn't know about. That was my interpretation.

"Did he have beer?" I asked. I felt tough for tossing out "beer" so nonchalantly, but also, more privately, like a poser.

I'd certainly never drunk beer, nor would I if somebody offered me one. Beer was nasty.

"He had beer *and* wine coolers *and* a bottle of gin from his parents' liquor cabinet," Cinnamon said. "But I don't think anyone drank the gin. According to Steffie."

"That is so stupid," Dinah said. She eased the milk from my feet and took a swig. She carefully wedged the carton back. "Don't they know how busted they could get for that? Plus it's bad for their livers."

"I highly doubt they drank enough to damage their livers," Cinnamon said. "Anyway, not everybody drank." She turned to me. "But Malena did, and Gail Grayson."

Gail Grayson was my nemesis from elementary school. She was the full-of-herself purple-bra-wearing new girl who came in and stole away my ex-BFF Amanda. And Malena . . . well, she was even worse than Gail. Malena was a longtime Westminsterite like Cinnamon,which meant I had the joy of meeting her at the beginning of the school year, when Dinah and I transferred over.

Malena had boobs, and she wasn't afraid to use them. She applied lipstick right there in class, in front of everyone. She wore sheer blouses over camisoles, which just barely met the dress code. She wore glittery hair clips from San Francisco that had swaying, jeweled bits dangling down. You couldn't even find hair clips like that in Atlanta.

"Did Amanda have anything to drink?" I asked. "Was she there?"

"Um . . . do you really want to know?"

"I don't know. Do I?"

"She was there, and she did drink, according to Steffie," Cinnamon said. "A peach wine cooler."

Dinah met my eyes. Unlike Cinnamon, she'd known the pre-junior-high Amanda. Sweet, smart Amanda with the heart-shaped freckles. Amanda who liked Cheetos. Amanda who used to make fun of people for being all snobby and superior and popular.

"Did she . . . get drunk?" I asked.

"Off one wine cooler? I don't *think* so," Cinnamon said. She was wiser than us in the way of alcohol because her brother, Carl, was a sophomore at the University of North Carolina. "She might not have even drunk it. Who knows? Maybe she just held it to look cool."

"So stupid," Dinah said.

I shifted my weight on the jungle gym, handing the milk to Cinnamon so I could let my legs dangle. "Is that the juicy part, that Gail and Malena and Amanda drank? Or is there more?"

"Why were they even there?" Dinah said. Out of all three of us, she probably felt the most threatened by the seventh grade popular girls, because she was the most different from them. Or maybe I was misreading? Maybe she wasn't threatened by them at all, for that very reason. Maybe I was the only one threatened?

"Because Brad invited them," Cinnamon said in a *duh* voice. "Because they're wild."

"Amanda didn't used to be wild," I said.

"She is now," Cinnamon said. "She kissed Alan Bauer in the hot tub."

"What?!" I cried.

"That's the juicy part," Cinnamon said, clearly pleased with my reaction.

"But Alan's an eighth grader—"

"So is Lars," she pointed out.

"—and he's not even cute. *Or* nice. He told Carmen De La Cruz she needed to wear deodorant!"

Cinnamon shrugged. "They kissed in the hot tub. That's what Steffie said."

"That is just *gross*," Dinah said.

Cinnamon downed the last of the milk, then dropped the carton through the bars of the play structure to the ground below. "Anyway, I just thought you should know, so you'd be prepared for Bryce's next weekend."

"Oh, God," I said. Bryce's parents were throwing a party for Bryce in celebration of the end of junior high. Well, the end of junior high for the eighth graders, since unlike us, they'd be moving on to high school. Bryce was an eighth grader. He was Lars's best friend. And because Lars was his best friend, Lars got to invite me. Which, when he called last week and told me, made me fizz up with happiness.

Now the fizziness turned to dread.

"Ah, it'll be fine," Cinnamon said. Now that she'd cranked up my worry, she switched gears and acted dismissive, as if I were making a bigger deal of it than necessary. I didn't know why Cinnamon liked to do that. "His parents are going to be there, right?"

"Right . . ." I said hesitantly.

"So that means no wine coolers. So you have nothing to worry about."

Dinah shook her head. "I'm glad I'm not going."

An expression crossed Cinnamon's face that told me she wished she was. I wished she was, too. Then I wouldn't be alone.

"You do know what this means, though, don't you?" she asked.

"That I'm destined for abject humiliation and a terrible outbreak of zits?" I said. "And I'll have to order Proactiv Solution from that infomercial? Which supposedly Kelly Clarkson uses, but somehow I'm thinking not really?"

"*No*," Cinnamon said. She looped her legs over the topmost bar on the jungle gym, swung upside-down, and dropped off. She didn't pick up the milk carton. "It means, my friend, that if Amanda can kiss Alan Bauer, *you* can kiss Lars. Finally and at last."

Dinah giggled, but didn't disagree.

Cinnamon looked up at me with her hands on her hips. "Winnie? Babe? It's time."

In the olden days, boys had to do all the work. They brought girls flowers; they held hands on charming wooden porch swings. Eventually, they made the bold move of kissing. The girls just had to be pretty and charming and demure.

Unfortunately, I was in no way demure. We didn't have a porch swing, and I preferred Junior Mints to roses.

But while the olden days may have had some perks, did I really want to return to a way of life when girls had to wear stockings and flutter their eyelashes? My feminist leanings might not be up to Sandra's standards, but of course I thought that every human should get to do what he or she wanted to do. Boys should be able to wear pink and play with dolls; girls could be tough and rowdy skateboarders or whatever.

But the truth of the matter was this: even with all that, even knowing that the olden days were long gone and that I was brave, independent Winnie who could do my own thing, I would still rather Lars make the first move and kiss *me*. I couldn't help it. I wanted romance and anticipation and a wonderful, beautiful moment to hold in my heart forever. We were talking first kiss here, for heaven's sake!

My first kiss, anyway.

Eeek! Had Lars kissed other girls before? Eeek eek eek!

Okay, let's think about the positives. Just say Lars *had* kissed a girl before. Or two or three or whatever, although the thought of him having kissed three different girls made my stomach flip. But in one way, that would be good, because he'd know what to do. I knew what to do in theory, but the only person I'd ever touched tongues with was Amanda, back in the second grade. Just our tips touched, just for a micro-second. It felt *extremely* weird, one wet tongue touching another. We'd also pricked our fingers and pressed them together, meaning she'd be my blood sister for always.

And now here she was frequenting hot tub parties and swigging wine coolers. Her first kiss had already happened. Probably lots more "firsts" that I wasn't even aware of.

So why don't you call her and ask for some tips? I thought. But I didn't truly consider it. Sometimes the brain just made words come into your head that in no way reflected reality. Amanda wasn't a buddy I could call out of the blue anymore. Weird and sad and true.

If Lars hadn't kissed anyone, that would be better. He would be my first, and I would be his. I didn't want other girls existing in his memory, anyway. Still, I wondered: Who *might* he have kissed? No seventh graders, surely. I scrolled through the set of eighth grade girls he sometimes hung out with: Taryn, who liked anime; Chloe, who was in French with us and who seemed chummy with him; Miranda, who liked *him*—that was obvious—but who wasn't pretty, so who cared?

Was I a bad person for thinking that?

Girls who weren't pretty were allowed to get kissed, too. Just not by Lars. *My* Lars.

I sighed. It wasn't even the middle of the day on Saturday, and already the weekend seemed too long. After leaving Memorial Park, Cinnamon had gone to a baseball game with her dad, and Dinah had returned to her house to read a book she was into. Something about vampires. So I'd gone back home, too. I'd crawled into bed and tried to go back to sleep, but that hadn't happened. Obviously, being in my own obsessive company wasn't working out that well for me.

So I got up off my butt and found Sandra and Bo lounging on a quilt in the backyard. It was just starting to get warm—yay spring!—and Sandra was wearing cutoffs. Her legs were pale.

I plopped down beside them. "Hi, guys," I said.

"Hey, Winnie-O," Bo said. He scooted over their Boggle game to give me more room. Bo and Sandra were in a Boggle phase, keeping a running tally of who was kicking whose fanny.

"Can I ask a question?" I said.

Sandra stretched. The silver ring Bo had given her gleamed on her index finger, making her look artsy. The stone in its center was a moonstone.

"What's up?" she said.

I was glad she was mellow. Otherwise I'd have backed off.

"Well . . ."

"Yessss?" Bo said.

"I was hoping we could discuss kissing."

"Oh, good God," Sandra said. "*Winnie.*"

I blushed, but the thing about Sandra and Bo (unless

Sandra was in one of her moods) was that I could blush around them and still keep going.

"I just don't understand what you do with your tongues," I said.

"How many tongues do you have?" Bo asked.

"Ha ha," I said. "One that belongs to me, one that belongs to someone else."

"And who might this someone else be?" Sandra said.

I looked at her. *She* knew.

"I'm serious," I said.

"You wiggle them around like this," Bo said. He stuck out his tongue like a little kid and went *bluh-buh-bluh-buh-bluh-buh*.

Sandra shoved him. "That's what you *used* to do, before I taught you the error of your ways."

Bo pretended he'd been sizzled. "Ouch!"

I laughed.

"Just . . . be subtle about it," Sandra told me. "You may not believe it, but it really will happen naturally, if you let it. But it's not a jam-down-the-throat thing—*ever*."

I nodded. No jamming down the throat.

"It's more . . . soft. Like saying 'hello,' and then having a whole conversation, only not with words." She glanced at Bo, and he held her gaze. There was something real in his eyes, something strong and true despite his constant teasing. How could I have ever thought they'd break up?

"Would you like a demonstration?" he asked.

"Bo!" Sandra protested.

He leaned forward and planted his lips on hers: *smack*. They toppled over, but he kept the kiss going. It made my "eek" feelings resurface, because it was such a personal thing to watch. And yet I did watch. My heart pounded, and my skin grew hot. Nervous giggles burbled out.

Bo released my sister, but only because she pushed him off. She sat up, flushed and trying not to smile, but not succeeding.

"Nice way to be a perv, Bo. You're going to scar her for life."

"Cause no other boy can live up to my extreme hunkiness?"

She snorted.

Bo grinned. "And that, little Winnie, is how you do it."

This was what I wore to Bryce's party when it finally rolled around: a denim miniskirt that fit really well as long as I was standing up (when I sat down, it required some yanking), a white T-shirt that was super faded and had a few splotches of paint on it from when Dad and I painted my dresser, and brown sparkly flip-flops. The miniskirt was to make my legs look good, and the paint-splotched T-shirt gave me a sexy, breezy kind of look. I hoped.

I painted my toenails sky blue and pink, alternating every other one. I put a flower decal on my right big toe and a butterfly on the left. I stroked my Rock Star glitter dust over my eyelids and applied clear gloss to my lips. I didn't put on actual lipstick, because A) it always looked weird, B) what if it got on my teeth, and C) even though I knew guys kissed girls wearing lipstick all the time, I couldn't get my head around it. Wouldn't it taste lipstick-y? Wouldn't it make the guy's lips pink or red or whatever?

It was the same problem I had imagining breast implants—not that I would *ever* get breast implants or any kind of plastic surgery. Ever, ever, ever (I thought it was important to make this promise to myself now, before I turned thirty and got saggy and fat).

But with breast implants, just like lipstick, surely they'd be too obvious, wouldn't they? Too un-real. Wouldn't a guy want to kiss your real lips? And feel your real . . . ?

Aye-yai-yai. Embarrassing!

But clear lip gloss was acceptable. It wasn't waxy, and it tasted like mango. Big thumbs-up.

"You look good," Sandra said in the car on the way to Bryce's. Sandra, not Mom, was dropping me off, and I needed to remember that the next time she annoyed me. Much cooler to be dropped off by your seventeen-year-old sister in her golf-ball-yellow Beemer than by your mom in her silver Volvo.

"Do I really, or are you just saying that?" I asked. I jerked on my skirt. "Am I, you know, being too skimpy?"

"Dude," she said, glancing at me from the driver's seat. Her look said *No, you aren't.* "There's no need to be a skank, 'kay? I'm proud of you for having taste."

I felt warm inside. She was my role model, after all:

sexy for sure in her battered jeans and thrift store button-downs.

We arrived at Bryce's house, and suddenly I didn't want to get out. There were people in there—real live eighth graders—and they would look at me. They would talk about starting high school, and I would be the loser seventh grader. I might be the only seventh grader! Maybe it would be better to stay in Sandra's slobby, pizza-smelling Beemer. *Ooo, yeah! We could go get pizza! Sandra loves pizza!*

"Hey, Sandra, you want to—"

"No. Get out," she said.

"You don't even know what I was going to say!"

She leaned over me and opened the door. "Off you go, baby bird. Fly away! Have fun!" She used her foot to shove my thigh, leaning against her own door for leverage.

"Sandra!" I protested. I couldn't believe she was *shoving* me out of the car. I scooted out quick so that no stray onlookers would see.

"Bye!" she called as she zoomed away.

Traitor fink evil sister. I would *not* remember her giving-me-a-ride kindness the next time I was annoyed with her after all. My heart pounded, and I could only hope that all the anger/embarrassment/adrenaline would give my cheeks a lovely glow. *Why, look at Winnie*, people would think. *How healthy! How vibrant!*

Well, nothing to do but bite the bullet, so I lifted my chin and walked confidently to Bryce's front door. *You are at the beach*, I said, my trick to get the proper saunter down. *You are strolling on the beach and you are happy, happy, happy.*

I lifted my hand to knock, but the door opened before my knuckles made contact.

"Winnie! *Hey!*" Steffie said. She knew me just barely from being Cinnamon's neighbor, though she stretched out the "hey" as if we were far closer. "I thought you were Farrin, but that's okay. Come on in!"

"Okay, cool!" I chirped. *Ugh. "Okay, cool"?! Okay, stupido. Okay, total dorky-o.*

"Lars is back there," Steffie said, pointing deeper into the house. That made me feel good, that she would know to connect me with him.

I wandered through the crowd, looking at all the skin, smelling all the perfumes and colognes. Ty had recently started wearing cologne. It was so cute. He was jealous of Mom's perfumes, so she got him this pine-scented spray-on cologne from the Body Shop. Whenever he used it, he puffed out his chest like a baby rooster.

An eighth grader named Cheri bumped into me and said, "Oops, sorry!" But she didn't look sorry. She pretty much didn't look at me at all.

I wished Cinnamon was here. Not Dinah, who would twitter and vibrate and smile in a petrified way. It would be excruciating. But Cinnamon would be an excellent party pal.

In the TV room, I spotted Lars playing a game on Bryce's Xbox. He was doing the full-body thing, holding the controller in front of him and lunging first to the right, then at full-tilt back to the left. He kept up a continuous back-and-forth with Bryce, throwing out phrases like, "Oh, yeah? Not so fast, loser!" and "Your ass is grass!"

He was very, very *boy*.

"Um, hi," I said, walking over and standing by the sofa.

Lars glanced away from the screen. His face broke into a smile. "Winnie! Hey, girl!"

Crashing sounds splattered from the TV, and Bryce leaned back and punched a fist into the air. "Yeah!" he crowed. "Take that, sucka!"

On the screen, a metallic blue car burst into flames.

"Oops," I said. I felt bad for making Lars lose, especially since Bryce was now up on his feet and doing a hip-circling, churn-the-butter victory dance.

"Oh *yeah*, I'm the *king*, oh *yeah*, I kicked your *boo*ty!" Those were his brilliant lyrics.

"Just getting your confidence up," Lars retorted, standing up and smacking Bryce's head. "C'mon, Win. Let's bounce."

Bryce hooted, and Lars smacked him again. He took my hand and pulled me away, and my insides soared. He was holding my hand! He was holding my *hand*!

"You found the place all right?" he asked as we walked.

I was really too hand-focused to answer, but I managed to nod. "Um, yeah. Well, Sandra did. She Mapquested it."

He nodded back. His fingers were strong. He was so incredibly adorable. "You, uh, want something to drink?"

It filtered into my consciousness that he'd led me to the

kitchen, where two liter bottles of soda lined the counter. Behind the counter was Bryce's mom, doing the serving.

"Sure," I said. Bryce's mom wouldn't spike the soda—not hardly. "A Sprite, please."

We chitchatted with Mrs. Thorton, and that was easy. The talk-politely-to-grown-ups thing was always easy for me.

"Well, check ya later, Mrs. T," Lars said—so cute! Mrs. T!—and the two of us went into the living room and stood by a wall. We drank our drinks. We smiled at each other. Lars moved his head to the music. Kids laughed and chattered, and from another room, I heard Steffie squeal. It was quite distinctive, her squeal. It was meant to make people notice.

"You want to go outside?" Lars asked.

"Sure," I said. I was Miss Ace Vocabulary, apparently. *Want to go bash your head in a wall? Sure!*

In the cool night air, I felt more normal. It was a more level playing field: less eighth graders, more nature. Or houses. Whatever.

"Kinda crazed in there," Lars said, squeezing my hand as we ambled into the Thortons' backyard. Darkness wrapped around us. "Sorry."

"No," I said. "It's a great party. It's sweet that Bryce's parents would throw it for him."

"You should have been at Brad's last weekend," he said. "Now that was *really* crazed."

"Oh, yeah?" He and I had never talked about it, so I played dumb and pretended Cinnamon hadn't given me the scoop.

"A lot of people got wasted. A couple of seventh graders, even."

I tried to gauge his opinion.

"You know that girl Amanda?" he asked. "Long, blond hair?"

"She used to be my best friend," I told him.

He seemed surprised. "For real?"

"Well . . . yeah." It was odd that he wouldn't know this piece of me. But he'd only met me this year, after Amanda and I had already gone our separate ways.

He shook his head. "She was trashed, man."

"Nuh-uh. *Amanda*?"

"Uh-huh. Guys were laughing at her."

Oh no. It alarmed me, this vision of Amanda that in no way matched the Amanda I knew. Cinnamon said she'd only had one wine cooler.

"Are you sure it was Amanda?" I asked. "Are you absolutely positive?"

"She's the skinny one, right?"

Compared to Gail and Malena, Amanda was definitely the skinny one. My hopes fell.

We reached a stone bench built into a wall at the far end of the yard. Lars sat down, and since I was still holding his hand, I sat down, too. He let go of my hand and put his arm around my shoulder. My pulse skyrocketed.

"She needs to watch out," he said. "If she's doing this now, what's she going to do in high school, you know?"

"Maybe it was a one-time thing," I said. "Maybe she wasn't really trashed. Maybe she was just pretending." I was babbling, and I wanted to stop. Even though I cared about Amanda, I didn't want to care right this very second.

Lars looked at me. His face was *right there*, inches from mine, and I knew this was it: the moment of the first kiss.

He leaned in. I giggled and drew back. My breathing grew shallow, and my heart drummed against my ribs, more out of nervousness than anticipation. Extreme, horrible, freak-out nervousness, the kind I occasionally experienced before having to give an oral presentation or introduce myself to a crowd of strangers.

Lars tried again. I turned my head from his. I didn't mean to—I *so* didn't mean to—but it was too much, being in the actual moment and thinking, *Oh, god, lips. His. Mine. Touching!*

An anxious laugh made a very strange sound coming out of me. I could feel my smile go rubbery.

He leaned in. I pulled back. He leaned in further. I did a bob and a duck maneuver. It was bad. Bad, bad, bad. And the worst part of all was the doubt creeping into his eyes. He thought I didn't want him to kiss me, but I did!

"Winnie?" he said.

"Yes?" I squeaked. My cheeks burned.

"Hold still."

He put his hand under my chin and bent his head toward

mine. I squeezed shut my eyes. My heart tried to jump out of my chest.

His lips touched mine. Soft. Warm. Hesitant, and then not so hesitant, while all the time I was privately spazzing out. I was doing it! It was glorious! It wasn't hard at all!

And then came the tongue. At first it was gross, like a slug. I recoiled, but his mouth followed mine. His tongue kept at it.

Before I knew it, the slug-ness stopped seeming so sluggish, and my tongue went peeping out to meet his. Ack! It was interesting. Thrilling. Overwhelming.

His arm slipped around my waist. He pulled me close. This beautiful boy was kissing me and holding me close, and we were outside, and there was a party, and noise drifted over to us from people doing their party things. Music. Laughter. Squeals.

Lars paused to regard me.

"Hi," he whispered.

"Hi," I whispered.

We smiled, goofy and happy. He leaned back in, and my lips parted to meet his.

I would never be "never been kissed" again.

June

AT TRINITY, where I went to elementary school, graduation meant whooping and hollering and spazzy running around. When I thought back to our sixth grade ceremony, Alex Plotkin—gross, with a deep red stain around his mouth from fruit punch—flashed into my mind. I don't know why I thought of Alex Plotkin. I certainly didn't intend to think of Alex Plotkin. Like I said, gross.

But. The point was, graduation at Westminster was a far more formal affair, even for us seventh graders. First came a ceremony in Pressley Hall, with presentations and awards and a song or two performed by the chorale. Then a baked chicken lunch served with cloth napkins and glass glasses, instead of the plastic ones with ridges we usually used. We dressed up in fancy clothes. Iced tea or water were our beverage choices. No fruit punch. And instead of running around afterward, we mingled and chatted politely to everyone's parents and grandparents and brothers and sisters.

And, if we were me, we also squeezed our feet as squish-small as we could inside our beautiful new shoes, even though the damage was already done and blisters were on the rise. (And we refer to ourselves as the "royal we," apparently. Which we found quite annoying and blamed fully on the endless graduation speeches. *"We're so pleased to announce . . ." "When we reflect upon this special occasion . . ." "We only wish we could say 'we' a thousand more times . . ."* Enough already!)

So. Right. If we were me—which I am! I'm me, yay!—I would wish very privately for a Band-Aid, or at least for a good old-fashioned paper napkin to fold into a rectangle and shove into the back of each shoe. I'd sworn to Mom they fit perfectly, because I'd wanted them so bad. But they didn't, and now they were killing me.

Un-yay.

"I'm just so proud of these girls!" Mrs. Taylor said to Mom. Mrs. Taylor's daughter was Louise, a fellow Trinity alum. Louise and I weren't exactly buddies, but we'd gone to school together forever, so we weren't *not* buddies, either. Louise was like a nubbly stuffed animal lying on the floor of the closet. I wouldn't throw it away, but I wouldn't care if my cat, Sweetie-Pie, used it as a chew toy and kicked at it with her hind legs.

"I'm proud, too," Mom said, putting her arm around my shoulder. Louise was off being flouncy with a girl named Trish, both of them angling for attention from a group of boys.

"They grow up so fast," Mrs. Taylor said, as if no one had said that one before. It was the theme of the day: *They grow up so fast. Time just flies, doesn't it? How is it possible that our babies have finished seventh grade?*

Ty sighed loudly and wormed his way between me and Mom. He was in that mood of leaning against everybody and refusing to bear his own weight.

"How long till we go?" he complained.

"Ten hours," I told him.

"Nuh-uh."

"A while," Mom said, nudging him off her leg. "Go lean on someone else."

"Can I have another brownie?"

"Sure," Mom said. "Get your dad one while you're at it. Find him and take it to him."

Ty weaved through the crowd to the dessert table, and Mrs. Taylor clucked.

"Such a sweet boy," she said.

"Sometimes," Mom said.

"Isn't he in Joseph Strand's class?" Mrs. Taylor said, her voice taking on an *isn't-it-tragic* tone. I stopped adjusting my shoe to listen.

"It breaks my heart," Mom said. Unlike Mrs. Taylor, she didn't sound fakey, which was one of the reasons I was glad to have her for a mother. And even though she often made eye-rolling remarks about all three of us kids, we knew she loved us to distraction.

"What breaks your heart?" I asked.

"A little boy in Ty's class," she said. "He has—"

"Winnie! Ellen!" Mrs. Wilson cried, breaking into our circle. Mrs. Wilson was Amanda's mother, and, like Amanda, she was beautiful. Both had Alice-in-Wonderland blond hair, although Mrs. Wilson's was chin-length, while Amanda's fell halfway down her back. Both had petite, curvy figures, the sort that made grown-ups tell Mrs. Wilson she looked twenty-five and made the junior high guys call Amanda "hot."

"Ellen, can you believe it?" Mrs. Wilson said. "Our little girls—starting eighth grade!"

"*Mom*," Amanda said. "We have three whole months first." I hadn't noticed her because it was so crowded, but there she was behind her mother, looking gorgeous and sylph-like in a long, black skirt and black cami. A "sylph" is a mystical creature kind of like a fairy, made mainly of air. I'd learned that from one of Dinah's fantasy books. Amanda had always been tiny, but lately she'd been looking downright wispy. She also wore a lot more eyeliner. Like, on purpose. Dark, thick lines not meant to be ignored.

"Hey, Amanda," I said.

"Hey, Winnie," she said.

It was so weird. I knew this person—I'd shared *blood* with this person—and yet here she was a stranger in front of me. Not a complete stranger . . . and yet not a battered stuffed animal, either. Louise was dismissible. Amanda? Never.

The grown-ups kept talking, and Amanda stepped to the side to disassociate herself from her mother. The tilt of her head prodded me to join her.

"So," she said. "Are you and Lars going to, you know, have a good summer?"

It surprised me that she knew about Lars. Then again, that was silly. I knew stuff about her.

"Actually," I said, "he's going to be in Prague all summer. His dad got a fellowship."

Amanda grimaced. "That sucks."

"I know." Lars had told me just last week, and my heart had plummeted. But I'd quickly sensed that I was more bummed about it than he was, so I'd tried to check my emotions. "Wow, Prague, that's so awesome," I'd said to him.

But it *did* suck. It totally sucked.

"So will you try to stay together?" Amanda asked.

"Of course!" I said without thinking. And then doubt crept in. Wouldn't we? What other option was there? Was Lars thinking there was some other option?

Amanda must have picked up on my worry, because she said, "Cool. You guys are cute together."

"Thanks," I said. I flashed to the Amanda-in-the-hot-tub story, but couldn't make it match up with the flesh-and-blood Amanda in front of me. Except *kind of* I could. I just didn't want to.

"Are you . . . seeing anybody?" I said, feeling immediately idiotic for the way my question came out. What was I, her grandmother?

Still, maybe the hot tub guy was her boyfriend. Maybe he wasn't then, but was now, and she'd had a crush on him and that's why she'd kissed him.

She shook her head and smiled wryly, like she was a loser. Which she was so not. She had to know that. But sometimes beautiful girls pretended otherwise, which I suppose was better than being snotty.

"Well . . ." I said.

We stood there. The silence stretched out, making my brain feel panicky.

"Your shoes are *gor*geous," she finally said. "Where'd you get them?"

"Saks," I told her, feeling a flush of pleasure. If Louise had complimented my shoes, I wouldn't have had the same reaction.

"I love them," she said.

Dinah and Cinnamon ran up, giddy and giggling. Each grabbed one of my arms.

"Winnie, you've got to see this," Cinnamon said.

"It's Alex Plotkin," Dinah said. "He's stuck in a high chair."

"He's stuck in a . . . what?"

"A high chair," Cinnamon said, yanking me so that I lunged forward.

I made a stab at resisting, because I felt rude for abandoning Amanda. But there were two of them and one of me—not to mention the promise of Alex in a high chair. I didn't know the cafeteria even had high chairs. Maybe the cafeteria ladies got them out just for graduation lunches?

"Um, guess I'll see you?" I said to Amanda.

"Bye, Winnie," she said as if she were amused. As if Dinah

and Cinnamon were laughable, as if seventh graders in high chairs had stopped being interesting years ago. It was the only glimpse I'd had, during this particular exchange, of her icky "popular" persona.

But I glanced over my shoulder as I was being dragged away, and her expression threw me. She didn't look condescending. She looked sad.

Lars and I met at the mall a couple of days later. He was flying to Prague the next morning, so this was our good-bye. He took me to California Pizza Kitchen for dinner. Well, actually we met there, since both of us had to be dropped off. Still, it was very date-ish.

Over Thai chicken pizza, we made small talk. I found myself picking at my food instead of digging in wholeheartedly like my normal piggy self, and I despised myself for it. I am *not* one of those girls who cares about weight and eats only salad and keeps the conversation focused on the boy and his interests because that's how to get a man.

But my stomach was tight, and eating seemed overly messy and complicated. Picking and nibbling proved easier.

Also—and this was something I didn't know how to make sense of—it was kind of seeming like maybe we didn't have so much to talk about, Lars and I. At least, not when we were away from school and our other friends. I despised myself for that, too. For not being better at all this. For not knowing how to just . . . get over myself.

"So," I started, determined to get our date on track. I

was not a boring blob. "In Prague, will you learn to speak . . ." My words tapered off as I realized I didn't know what language Prague people spoke. Well, not Prague people. Praguians?

"Czech," Lars supplied. He took the last slice of pizza. "I don't know, maybe a little. But we'll only be there for three months."

Three months, right. *Only* three months.

"I hope there will be some other American kids there," he went on. "Or not even American, just kids who speak English. Someone to hang out with."

"Maybe you'll meet some British kids," I said. "Or Australian! Eh, mate?"

He grinned. I loosened a little.

"Australia rocks," he said. "Did you know they have wombats?"

"Plus the most poisonous species of jellyfish in the world." I'd read it in Ty's *National Geographic Kids* magazine. "If you get stung by one, you're dead in forty seconds."

Lars ripped off a bite of pizza, shaking his head. "Man. I wish we were going to Australia instead of Prague."

"But Prague'll be fun, too," I said, sort of hoping he'd disagree.

He chewed and swallowed. "Yeah, I hear you. Getting to see any part of the world is cool."

I sighed. He was right: it would be cool. I was the uncool one, needy and sad.

He reached over and touched my face. "I wish you were going to be there, though."

"Really?" My pulse raced. He touched my face! In the California Pizza Kitchen!

He grinned and tossed some bills on the table. "Ready to get out of here?"

I fumbled for my wallet. "Do you want me to . . . I mean, can I . . ."

"Your money's no good here, babe," he said.

"*Babe*?" I said.

He laughed. So did I. He stood up, grabbed my hand, and pulled me out of the booth. "Let's go. Aren't we supposed to meet your sister soon?"

But Sandra wasn't due to pick me up for almost an hour, which I was pretty sure he secretly knew. He led me to the outside parking deck, and he kissed me behind a concrete pillar. And kissed me and kissed me. My back pressed against the cool concrete. His lips were soft. He tasted like Thai peanut sauce.

In Sandra's Beemer, I asked her whether Lars and I would make it. I wanted her to reassure me that everything would be the same, only better, when he returned.

"Winnie, you're in seventh grade," Sandra said, as if that was some kind of answer.

"Not anymore," I replied.

She rotated her iPod dial and selected her "Mellow Yellow" playlist. Was this her way of telling me to chill? I *wanted* to chill. I wasn't being unchill on purpose. Didn't she get that?

"If what you guys have is real, it'll last," she told me. "If not, it won't."

"Gee, thanks."

She shot me a look. "But worrying about it will only make things worse. You can't be desperate, Winnie."

"I know!"

"I'm just saying."

"I *know*." My lips felt puffy from kissing. I loved that feeling. I gazed out the open window and wondered if Lars was thinking about me the way I was thinking about him.

After we got home, I tried to distract myself by watching *Hannah Montana* with Ty. Ty had a crush on the main girl, who went by the name "Miley" in her normal life, but was secretly a pop star named Hannah Montana. "Miley" was a cute name, I thought. So much cuter than "Winifred." "Winnie" was acceptable . . . but *Winifred*?

If I were a pop star, I could change my name to "Wiley." Except that was the name of the coyote on Bugs Bunny—so maybe not. Plus, it wasn't cute. Why was "Miley" cute, but not "Wiley"?

If I were a pop star, I would never worry about being boring or blobby. If I were a pop star, I wouldn't worry about Lars coming back to me or not. I'd know he would.

On the screen, Miley's annoying brother, Jackson, made

his belly button talk, which made Ty laugh. It was Ty's start-off-real-and-then-turn-fake laugh, which he did when he wanted to keep the hilarity going. I loved that about Ty, that laughing was so fun for him that he made more and more burble out.

"I want to do that with my belly button," he said.

"Okay, you're allowed," I said.

"And I want to learn how to make stink noises with my armpit, like Joseph. Joseph can make really good stink noises."

Joseph. Wasn't he the kid Mom and Mrs. Taylor had been talking about during our graduation luncheon? Something bad, something that broke Mom's heart. I'd meant to ask her about it, but had forgotten.

"Don't you, Winnie?"

"Huh?"

"Wish you could make stink noises."

I did, actually. There were several things like that I wished I could do: raise one eyebrow; pop my elbow out like Cinnamon, who was double-jointed; make my scalp wiggle; whistle through two fingers. I wouldn't mind being able to do a split, either. A split would be impressive, even if I was never a cheerleader.

What *could* I do in terms of weird body stuff? I could curl my tongue (easy), and I could bend each of my fingers from the top knuckle without letting the middle knuckle move. I taught myself that one with lots of practice, mainly during fifth grade social studies. With all ten fingers bent like that, I'd hold my hands out like claws and make zombie sounds, letting my face muscles go slack. Amanda used to giggle and shriek as I lurched toward her.

I could also sit in the lotus position with each foot on top of the opposite thigh. That one, like the tongue-curling, was easy for me.

"Can you do this?" I asked Ty, leaning back against the sofa and pretzeling my legs into lotus position *without even using my hands*. Talk about impressive.

Ty was intrigued. He tried, but his legs went into normal criss-cross-applesauce mode.

"Nope," I said. I unfurled my legs and stood up. "Keep working. You'll get it."

"Will you give me a dollar if I do?"

"No. Will you give me a dollar since I already can?"

"I'll give you a dollar if you give me a dollar."

"Sure, Ty, whatever."

I went and found Mom in the kitchen. She was making cookies, and the smell of vanilla was heavenly. Such a funny thing, vanilla: it smelled fabulous, but tasted good only once it was mixed up with other things like sugar and eggs and all that. Same with coffee, except its mixer-uppers were sugar and milk.

"Hey. Mom. What's up with that kid Joseph, from Ty's class?" I asked.

"Oh," Mom said. Her eyes softened around the edges.

"Well, Joseph's got leukemia. His parents just recently found out."

Leukemia? There was a girl who went to camp with me last year who'd had leukemia. Her name was Jessica. But by the time I knew her, she was fine.

"That's so sad," I said. "But kids get better from leukemia, right?"

"Usually," she said. "There's a lot that can be done, like chemo, which Joseph's going to start this summer."

Chemo for a six-year-old. Wow. "Will he lose his hair?"

She nodded. "Yeah, poor kid."

Her expression was sad, and I knew that in addition to feeling worried for Joseph, she was thinking about Ty. I was, too. I was thinking how awful it would be if Ty had a scary disease. If he had to go through chemo and lose all his hair before probably—but not definitely—being healed.

And here I was feeling sorry for myself because my boyfriend was traveling the world.

I was a turd.

"But he'll be okay," I insisted. "Joseph will be okay."

Mom used her wrist to push back her hair. She left a streak of flour across her forehead. "Sweetie, there just aren't any guarantees. But I sure hope so."

Morning came, and I awoke with the knowledge that Lars and his parents were traveling to the airport at that very moment to catch their early international flight. At ten o'clock, I thought, *Well, Lars is on the plane now*. He'd fly to Paris, which took nine hours, and then he'd catch a connecting flight to Prague. The Atlanta-to-Paris leg involved flying over the ocean. *Please don't let the plane crash*, I prayed.

I tried to be a better person and not be needy and pathetic. I tried to remember that my boy troubles (which weren't even *troubles* so much as a minor three-month-long inconvenience) weren't the most important thing in the world.

It kind of worked. I made plans to go to the pool with Cinnamon later in the week. Dinah called and reminded me that at least my boyfriend wasn't a vampire, which was indeed something to be thankful for.

As I lay in bed that night, I thought about Lars, far off in the universe and doing who-knew-what. Was he in Prague yet? Was he eating? Unpacking? Sleeping? I realized I didn't even know what the time difference was between us.

I also thought about Joseph. I could place him in my mind now: a skinny little guy who always wore cordoroys. Brown hair. Sweet smile. Ty had gone to his birthday party two months ago, and I'd accompanied Mom when she dropped him off. Joseph had come barreling out the front door wearing a gold eye patch, with a black patch for Ty in his hand. It was a pirate party. Later, Ty had come home with gold-coin treasure.

I wished I could make Joseph's leukemia go away. Same for anyone else who had cancer or a brain tumor or that crazy disease where you can't go out in the sunlight. I wished

I could make all the pain and sadness in the whole world go away. But I couldn't.

Something came into my head that I *could* do, though. Locks of Love. Sandra had a friend who'd done that. She'd grown her hair super long and then clipped it off for Locks of Love, so it could be made into a wig for a kid with cancer.

I imagined going to school with suddenly short hair and all the attention I'd get. I knew that wasn't the point. . . . though if people *did* ask why I'd done it, I didn't think it would be overly braggy to explain. I'd be modest about it, of course. But more importantly, I'd be helping someone in need.

I thought about all that for a long time. It was a satisfying place for my mind to hang out, nice and hopeful and warm with potential. And then I had the one-step-further thought that I could truly do it. Not just think about it, but *do* it. Chop off that hair—*whomp*!

Aye-yai-yai. Would I look good with short hair? Would I be able to survive without the option of a ponytail? Would I still be pretty?

Still . . . how cool it would be to be someone who wasn't afraid of such things. Who saw the need for something and did it, just like that.

I slid out of bed and padded to my computer, which Mom and Dad had gotten me when my homework assignments started getting harder and I was required to do more Internet research. They set up all sorts of parental controls, and they made me promise not to have "inappropriate e-mail or IM conversations." Yeah, yeah, yeah.

I hit the space bar to wake up the screen, clicked on Firefox, and typed in "Locks of Love." I learned that the wigs were actually called "hair prosthetics," which would have made me giggle, if not for the pictures on the site. I *had* hair, unlike the kids in the photo gallery who were stark, raving, no-doubt-about-it bald. Grinning, for the most part, but bald. Next to each bald picture was an "after" picture of the same kid wearing a hair prosthetic. Humans did look better with hair. I wouldn't argue with anyone on that one.

I scrolled further through the site and learned that in order to donate your hair, the cut-off part had to be ten inches long from tip to tip. I dug a ruler out of my desk, tilted my head sideways, and measured from my part to the ends. Fifteen inches! I could donate tomorrow!

Except, wait. If I cut ten inches off, that would leave me with only five inches. I felt selfish for caring with those bald kids smiling out at me, but five inches wasn't a lot of hair.

I used the ruler again to see what my hair measured from my part to my chin. Eight inches. So if I wanted to be left with chin-length hair, I'd need to grow my hair out to a total length of eighteen inches. Eighteen minus fifteen meant I had three inches left to go. In hair time, that equaled approximately half a year.

Well.

I put the ruler back.

It was disappointing not to get to do something right this very second to make the world a better place (and me a better Winnie). And unlike the graduation-day mothers with their cries of "Oh me, oh my, time goes by so fast," I knew that time was far more likely to creep along like a very sluggish snail, especially if you were waiting for something particular to happen.

But that was okay. I could handle it. Someone with leukemia might not have all the time in the world, but, as far as I knew, I did.

July

Ah, summer. Even without Lars, I couldn't help but love the hot, lazy, glorious days. Sleep in, eat a little brekkie (my fun new way of saying "breakfast"), watch a rerun of *Dawson's Creek* on the Lifetime channel, or sometimes an episode of *Flight 29 Down* with Ty. *Flight 29 Down* was about a group of kids who survived a plane crash, but were now stuck alone on an island, trying to survive. It was dorky, with lots of life lessons about teamwork! And cooperation! And never giving up despite the odds! Even so, I found myself getting sucked in.

Plus, ever since accepting Cinnamon's invitation to go on a weekend camping trip (just me, 'cause Dinah was off to her grandparents), I'd been boning up on my outdoor wilderness skills. Which weren't many. But I figured watching the Flight 29 kids had to count for something.

On a normal day, after a relaxing morning of TV, I'd go for a bike ride or meet Cinnamon and Dinah at the pool. Something to get me off my butt and out into the world. At some point I'd fit in a lunch of PB&J, Doritos, and a Coke, or occasionally a pizza Hot Pocket from the pool's snack bar—

although they were gross, and every time I ordered one, I swore to myself I'd never order one again. Maybe they'd be decent if they were cooked in a toaster, but the snack bar workers nuked them in the microwave, which made the crust all nasty.

But today was not a normal day. Today Mom dropped me off at Cinnamon's house with my duffel bag and my Snoopy sleeping bag, which Cinnamon laughed at. She'd also laughed at my sneakers, which apparently marked me as a greenhorn. She *also* laughed when I brought up *Flight 29 Down*.

"That's not real camping," Cinnamon said, even though she'd never seen the show. She shoved a pair of wool socks into her backpack. "We will not be foraging for food, and we will not be building a shelter out of palm leaves, I promise. Which I highly doubt six kids could do, anyway. And how come only the kids survived the plane crash and no grown-ups?"

"Don't ask me. Ask the script writers," I said.

"Exactly. *Script* writers, because it's not real." She yanked shut her backpack's zipper. "Real camping is campfires and tents and s'mores. Have you ever had a real s'more? A *real* s'more?"

I thought about Ty and his microwaved marshmallows, spinning round and round until the timer dinged. Unlike Hot Pockets, marshmallows did quite well in the microwave. Smack them between two graham crackers with half of a Hershey bar stuck in between, and wa-la. Instant deliciousness.

"They can't be that different," I said.

"You are sadly mistaken," Cinnamon said. "Just wait and see."

A car horn beeped.

"That's her!" Cinnamon cried.

Excitement fluttered in my stomach, and I followed Cinnamon downstairs. This would be my first time to go camping *and* my first time to meet Cinnamon's mom. I'd heard a lot about her—she smoked, she made silver jewelry, she used to hate Cinnamon's stepmom, but had mellowed slightly since getting a boyfriend of her own—but we'd never met face-to-face. Mrs. Meyers lived in North Carolina, which was where we'd be going camping. From Atlanta it would take three hours to get there.

"Hi, Mom!" Cinnamon said as she burst out the back door. Cinnamon tended to talk about her mom dismissively, but she sure seemed happy to see her. "This is Winnie. Winnie, Mom. Mom, Winnie."

"Hi, Winnie," Mrs. Meyers said. She'd gotten out of her Subaru and was in the process of opening the trunk. She was way skinnier than Cinnamon, with grayish-blond hair pulled into two pigtails. Her jeans were patched with purple and red squares. She wore chunky silver rings on seven of her ten fingers.

"Hi, Mrs. Meyers," I said.

"Call me Mary Beth," she urged.

"Told you," Cinnamon said.

Cinnamon's dad came out with my bag, which he loaded into the car along with Cinnamon's backpack.

"Mary Beth," he said.

"Warren," she said.

They were civil to each other, but nothing close to friendly. Mr. Meyers walked over and hugged Cinnamon good-bye. He released her, but kept his hands on her shoulders. "Listen up, you. You better take care of yourself, and you want to know why?"

"Da-a-ad," she complained.

He refused to be deterred. "Because you're my one and only brown-haired, green-eyed daughter. I want you back safe and sound." He turned to me. "That goes for you, too."

"Yes sir," I said.

"Even though your eyes are brown."

"And I'm not your daughter."

"Right," he said, grinning.

Cinnamon and I climbed into the car, and we were off.

The first two-thirds of the journey was smooth and easy, but the last hour took us higher into the Blue Ridge Mountains, and while it was gorgeous, it was also extremely curvy. The two-lane road took us through an abandoned work zone called Bad Creek Project, which looked industrial and spooky, then snaked up endless hairpin turns that made me green-in-the-gills carsick. To our right, bare rock stretched toward the sky. To our left, the road dropped off sharply into forest.

"You should come up in the winter," Cinnamon said from the front seat. She twisted to face me. "Icicles hang from the rocks, like three feet long. Sometimes we stop and break them off."

"Mother Nature's popsicles," Mary Beth said.

"Remember the time Logan stuck one in his diaper?" Cinnamon asked.

Mary Beth chuckled.

I was probably supposed to ask who Logan was, but I wasn't in a good position to be talking. If I opened my mouth, I was afraid I might throw up.

"Logan's one of the kids who's coming camping with us," Cinnamon supplied. "He's eight now. His brother, Adam, is our age."

I gave a tiny nod.

"The Gibsons are *very* nice," Mary Beth said. "We've been going camping with them since before Cinnamon's father turned into a jerk."

"Mom!" Cinnamon said.

"You're right, you're right," she said. "He was a jerk all along. I was just too dumb to realize it."

"*Mom.*"

If this was the "slightly mellow" version of post-divorce Mary Beth, then I felt bad for Cinnamon. Except I was too queasy to care.

Cinnamon crossed her eyes at me. Then she frowned. "Winnie? You okay?"

I wasn't, but I didn't want her drawing attention to it.

"Mom, Winnie's carsick," she announced.

"Oh, poor thing," Mary Beth said. We took a sharp turn, and I gripped the armrest. "Do you need me to stop?"

"That's okay," I managed.

"Good, because we're almost there," Cinnamon said. "Aren't we, Mom? Aren't we almost to the 'Are You Lost' rock? And from there it's, like, twenty minutes to the campsite."

"There it is," Mary Beth said, pointing. I wanted her to put her hand back on the steering wheel, so I obediently lifted my head. A gray rock the size of a grizzly bear protruded from the mountain side, painted with crude white letters which read, R U LOST, OR R U SAVED?

Cinnamon leaned forward to peer out the windshield, then flopped back into her seat. The car bounced.

"I love that rock," she said. Even through my nausea, I could hear how happy she was. Happy to be with her mom, happy to be going camping, happy to have me along.

She turned to face me yet again, and I didn't get how she could squirm about so much and *not* feel sick. Her grin dimmed as she took in my condition. Then it flashed back, both sympathetic and superior.

"City girl," she said condescendingly.

I couldn't defend myself. I was too weak to reply.

•••

At the campsite, Mary Beth had us unload the trunk and put the plastic milk jugs in the creek to keep them cold. Cinnamon showed me how to loop a piece of twine through each jug's handle and leash them to a tree so they couldn't float away. They looked goofy, like bobbing-milk dogs. I thought it was a cool idea, though—way more funky than a red-and-white insulated cooler.

The Gibsons arrived as we were putting up our tents—one tent for Mary Beth, one tent for me and Cinnamon, both of them army green and un-fancy. Our fellow campers piled out of their Honda Odyssey with lots of noise and laughter, and the first thing Cinnamon said to them was, "Hey, guys! This is my friend, Winnie. She got carsick."

I blushed. I didn't like it when Cinnamon said things like that, and she said them fairly often. To Mr. Fackler, when I was late to history: *Don't be mad at her—her spaghetti gave her the runs.* To the annoying Louise, after Louise said something rude about a girl who supposedly had bad personal hygiene: *You think that's bad? Sometimes Winnie goes three days without taking a shower!* To Lars, taking over my computer when I was IM-ing him: *winnie misses u so much! omg! she's like totally whipped!*

Sometimes it felt like she was out to get me. Or at least make me feel dumb. But she was also one of my BFFs, and I knew that in my heart. So it was confusing.

Logan, the younger of the two Gibson boys, said, "Gross. Did she barf?" He glanced at me in the way of eight-year-old boys, loud and show-off-y and not the slightest bit sympathetic. *Icicle-diaper boy*, I thought.

The older boy, Adam, shoved his brother. "Nice way to make a first impression," he said. To me, he said, "Ignore him. He still watches the *Doodlebops*."

"I do not!" Logan yelped.

I smiled. The Doodlebops were an Australian kid-music band with fluorescent hair and overly-animated expressions, and no self-respecting eight-year-old would ever be caught watching them. Even Ty, at six, knew enough to scorn the Doodlebops.

"She didn't barf, but she came close," Cinnamon said, wanting to swing the attention back to her.

"Because you made me ride in the back," I said. "If I'd ridden in the front, I'd have been fine."

"Yeah, Cinnamon," Adam said. He had dark brown hair, cut kind of geekily, and brown eyes. "You should have let her have the front."

Cinnamon considered this. Then she shrugged. "Oops."

Mrs. Gibson, who had fiery red hair and wore a blue sweat suit, dug around in the back of the Odyssey and emerged with a bottle of wine. "It's wine o'clock, sweeties!" she caroled. "Mary Beth, please tell me you remembered a corkscrew?"

"Wine?" Cinnamon said. "You're letting us have wine?"

"Ha ha," Cinnamon's mom said. She fished a corkscrew out of her pack and tossed it to Mrs. Gibson. "You kids are on dinner duty. Call us when it's ready."

"Ohhh, so that's how it's going to be," Cinnamon said.

The cork popped out with a satisfying *thwop*. "Yep," Mary Beth said.

She and Mrs. Gibson laughed, and Mr. Gibson, who looked a bit like an egg, brought over three plastic cups. They dropped down onto a log that had clearly lived by the fire circle for years and years.

"Ahh," Mr. Gibson said, pouring the wine. "Here's to good, clean living." The three of them raised their cups.

Adam turned to Cinnamon and said, "Pizza bagels?"

"Aces," Cinnamon said. "Me and Winnie'll start the fire."

By the time we'd eaten and cleaned up, it was dark. The fire popped and shimmered, and as I stared at the flames, I felt as if I were going into a trance. My muscles were sore and my belly was full, and watching the fire was as good as watching TV. Better, even. Magical.

The only problem was the smoke, which followed me no matter where I went. If I sat by Cinnamon on the log, the smoke found me there. When I scooched two feet to the left, the smoke scooched as well. When I got up and moved to a pig-shaped stump (which Adam informed me was indeed called "the pig"), the smoke faltered for a minute, then murmured, "Oh, there she is," and curled on over.

"It's chasing me!" I complained.

"It is not," Cinnamon said. "You just think it is because it keeps shifting to wherever you're sitting."

I gazed at her. "And the difference is . . . ?"

Adam laughed. It was a nice laugh, though like his hair, a bit on the dorky side. I'd learned over the course of the night that he was going into eighth grade, too. He went to a public school in Asheville, and we'd talked a little about the whole public school/private school thing. Like how Westminster's cafeteria food was actually good, while Adam's cafeteria still supported the "ketchup is a vegetable" rule. Also how not every single person at Adam's school cared about grades and status and going to the right college, which sounded refreshingly relaxing. So there were points in both schools' favor.

I also learned that Adam played the trombone, and that he was a boy scout. That's where he'd learned to make the pizza bagels, which were yummy.

I couldn't be certain—after all, I'd known him for less than three hours—but I got the strangest prickly sensation that he . . . I don't know. Kind of thought I was cute, maybe. Just from the way he checked my reaction when he said things, and from how he thwacked Logan's head when Logan laughed at me for jumping at a noise from the woods.

"She thought it was a bear!" Logan crowed.

"No, I didn't," I lied.

"Shut up," Adam told his brother. "She's never been camping before."

"Yeah I have," I said. "I went to spend-the-night camp last summer."

"Not the same," Cinnamon said.

"Don't worry, there are no bears in Pisgah Forest," Adam told me.

"Only escaped *murderers*," Logan said, stretching the word out.

"What?" I said.

Adam thwacked Logan again. "Murderer, singular," he corrected, meeting my eyes in apology. "Not murder*ers*."

"*What*?!" I cried.

"Mom, is there an escaped murderer in the forest?" Cinnamon called to Mary Beth, who was sitting across the fire and chatting with Mr. and Mrs. Gibson.

"No, of course not," Mary Beth said.

"Actually, yes," Mrs. Gibson said. "We heard it on the news."

"Told you!" Logan said.

"But it's nothing to worry about," she said. "Apparently, a convict from the state prison—"

"A *murderer*," Logan interjected.

"—broke free from his work group. The police think he headed up the Blue Ridge Parkway into the forest."

"Oh my god," Mary Beth said. "Should we be here? Is it safe?"

"Of course it's safe," Mrs. Gibson said. "He's not out to bother anyone. He just didn't want to be in jail."

"Can you blame him?" Mr. Gibson said, letting out a booming laugh. He leaned forward and lowered his voice. "Killed his wife. Crime of passion."

"Are you pulling my leg?" Mary Beth said. "I'm serious, Charlie. Tell the truth."

"No, no, it's absolutely true," Mrs. Gibson said. Her wide eyes didn't seem capable of deceit. She swayed a little, and Mr. Gibson steadied her. "But if he was in this neck of the woods, I'm sure it would be *crawling* with police."

"Unless he killed them all," Logan pointed out.

Adam thwacked him.

"Ow!" Logan said.

Mrs. Gibson patted Mary Beth's knee, then poured herself another cup of wine. "Now. Who's ready for s'mores?"

That night, in our tent, I tried not to think about the murderer. I giggled with Cinnamon about what a greedy-guts Logan was (he'd wolfed down four s'mores and five additional marshmallows), and agreed that her patented marshmallow-toasting technique beat the pants off Logan's scorch-'em-and-scarf-'em method.

"It's all about the coals," Cinnamon pontificated. Our hands were under our heads. Our sleeping bags were pulled up to our chins. "Stick your marshmallow directly in the fire, and it's going to burst into flames. Case closed."

"I hear ya," I said. Time after time, Logan had charred his marshmallows to a crisp, and time after time, he'd yelped in dismay and blown at them madly, which only fed the flames. But he'd eaten them anyway, blackened crust and all.

Adam, on the other hand, demonstrated admirable finesse.

His marshmallows puffed to perfection and turned an even, golden brown. Had there been a marshmallow-toasting prize, I secretly would have awarded it to him.

Adam was an interesting guy. Although, hmm . . . was that actually true? He was smart and said funny things and was somehow less stud-muffin-poser-ish than most boys I knew. Maybe it was a public school–versus–private school thing. Maybe private school guys were more polished, and not always in a good way.

But if I were honest with myself, the really interesting thing about Adam was that he liked *me*. It was both foreign and thrilling to have this boy whom I'd only known for several hours pay so much attention to me.

It wasn't like Adam was any competition for Lars. Not hardly. But was I the type of girl who not just one but two boys could like?

Apparently, I was.

Next to me, Cinnamon sighed. We listened to the silence, which wasn't really silence, since there were *things* out there, alive and moving on the other side of our flimsy tent. A twig snapped, and I flinched.

"You okay?" Cinnamon said.

"Yeah. You?"

"Yeah, yeah, sure. Only . . ."

"Only what?"

"You're going to kill me."

"Why?"

She rolled to face me. Her expression was pleading. "I have to pee."

"What? No!" I said. Everyone else was in their tents, probably asleep. The fire was out, doused by lugged-up jugs of creek water. It was dark and spooky and the murderer I was trying very hard not to think of leered and beckoned in my brain.

Come, little girlies, he whispered. *Come to me now.*

"Can't you hold it?" I said.

"I can't," Cinnamon said.

"Are you *sure*?"

"If I wait much longer, I'll go in the tent. And that would not be pleasant."

I scowled and pushed myself to my elbows. "Fine," I groused. "Let's go."

"Thank you, Winnie," she gushed, squirming out of her sleeping bag. "You are the best friend *ever*. And if you ever have to go, even in the middle of the night, I *promise* I'll go with you."

"You better."

"I will!"

We held hands as we tiptoed past the fire pit. Our grips tightened as an owl hooted. We fought to hold in our nervous laughter.

"Curse you, oh owl!" Cinnamon whispered.

"Demon of the dark!" I contributed.

"Don't say that word," Cinnamon said.

"What, 'demon'?"

"Yes! Don't!"

"Demon, demon, demon!" I whispered. It was funny. It was also payback for the "Winnie got carsick" remark.

"I'm serious!" Cinnamon begged.

We stepped behind a tree just a few feet from the campsite, and Cinnamon tugged down her sweatpants. She squatted, and after a few seconds I heard the *ssss* of pee against ground. If it were daylight, she'd have hiked much farther away to do her business. But in the pit of night? No way.

She did a shake-and-wiggle (no toilet paper) and yanked up her sweats.

"Okay, let's go," she said.

A moan came from the campsite. Cinnamon and I clutched each other, our fingers digging deep.

"What was that?" she said.

"I don't know!" I replied.

The moan came again, guttural and thick. My heart pounded.

"Omigod, omigod, omigod," Cinnamon babbled. "We're going to die!"

This wasn't a joke. This was real. My brain knew that something had to be done—we had to go to the campsite and help whoever was being hurt—but my body was frozen.

"Help!" I tried to say. It came out as a squeak. "*Help*!"

There was the ripping sound of a zipper being unzipped. "What's going on?" Mr. Gibson demanded.

Then everything happened fast. Cinnamon and I ran

toward Mr. Gibson, who'd trained his flashlight on Adam and Logan's tent. Through the fabric, I made out a dark hunched figure. The moan came again, a violent retching sound.

"Charlie, get the ax!" Mrs. Gibson screeched, pushing out of her tent. She wore a short pink nightie, and her hair was in curlers. "The ax! The ax!" She ran to the makeshift kitchen area and rooted frantically through a bag of canned goods.

"Get out of here, you maniac!" she shrieked. She threw a can of corn at her sons' tent, only her aim was terrible, and Mr. Gibson flung up his hands.

"Judy, watch it!" Mr. Gibson barked.

A growl came from the tent. A crazy escaped-convict's growl.

Omigod, I thought. *Somebody is going to die. I am standing right here, and somebody is going to die.*

I spotted the ax by the pig stump. I grabbed it, stumbling forward and lifting it above my head.

"Winnie!" Cinnamon screamed.

I reached the tent just as Logan tumbled out. He was green—way greener than I'd been on the drive through the mountains. He doubled over, and an arc of vomit streamed through the air. There was splattering. It was bad.

I dropped the ax, which thudded to the ground. When I saw it there, its blade dense and sharp, I felt lightheaded.

"Winnie, are you okay?" Cinnamon asked, rushing to my side.

"Too . . . many . . . marshmallows," Logan muttered. He swiped his mouth with the back of his hand. Then he threw up again.

"Eww!" Cinnamon said, jumping back.

Cinnamon's mother emerged from her tent. "Oh, God," she said, looking hung-over. "Is that vomit I smell?" She clapped her hand to her mouth.

Finally, out staggered Adam from the boys' tent. His hair was disheveled. He took in the scene—his parents, the vomit, me. The ax. His bleary eyes met mine.

"Wow," he said. "You private school girls are tough."

The next morning we packed up camp and drove to a hotel. A lovely Holiday Inn, with running water and toilets and an absence of deranged lunatics. Well, except for us.

The grown-ups paid for three rooms: one for Mr. and Mrs. Gibson, one for Mary Beth, and one for the four kids.

"No hanky-panky," Mrs. Gibson warned, which made us crack up.

"Yeah, right," Cinnamon said under her breath. "Who exactly would we have hanky-panky *with*?"

Adam blushed and glanced at me. I liked it.

Logan spent most of the morning in the bathroom, and Cinnamon, Adam, and I watched Showtime and bounced on the beds. We joked about the Great Ax Incident. We rapped on the bathroom door and asked Logan if he wanted us to bring him more marshmallows.

At wine o'clock, Adam, Cinnamon, and I swam in the pool while the grown-ups sipped chardonnay at the outdoor bar. Cinnamon begged her mom to buy us virgin piña coladas, but Mary Beth waved her off.

"Go get some exercise," she prodded.

"What about Logan?" Cinnamon said, gesturing at the chaise longue where Logan sprawled. "He's not exercising."

"Go exercise, Logan," Mr. Gibson said. "Give us a couple hundred laps."

Logan groaned.

Mrs. Gibson swatted her husband's arm. "Don't tease him. His tum-tum hurts."

There was another family swimming in the pool along with us. A dad, a mom, and a whole bunch of pale, skinny kids. One of the girls wore a gymnastics leotard for a bathing suit.

"Listen up, you rats," the dad bellowed. All his kids were in the shallow end. Two of them looked his way; the others kept listlessly splashing. The girl in the leotard bobbed in endless circles. "I'll pay any one of you ten dollars to go down the slide headfirst." He gestured toward the twisty slide in the deep end. "Headfirst, and on your back. Ten dollars. Any takers?"

The two paying attention shook their heads. The girl in the leotard wiped a slime booger from her nose.

"I'm talking ten big ones!" the dad tried again. "What's wrong with you kids?"

His wife said, "Frank."

"They're a bunch of wussies," he told her. He turned back to the pool. "You're all a bunch of wussies!"

"Hey, mister!" Cinnamon called. She grabbed my hand and raised it. "She'll do it!"

"What?" I yelped.

"If you can stand up to an ax-murderer, I think you can go headfirst down a slide," she said.

"*You* do it," I said.

"No way. It's got to be you."

"Oh, God," Adam said, hiding his face.

"Well?" the man said.

I looked at him. I looked at his kids, who'd suddenly grown interested. I looked at the slide, which wasn't *that* steep.

"Fine," I said. I clambered out of the pool and marched to the slide. I climbed the ladder.

"On your back!" the man called. "Headfirst on your back!"

I rolled my eyes. He obviously didn't know who he was dealing with. I turned down and squatted, clinging to the plastic edges. I scooched my rear end forward and stretched out on my back. The sky was a brilliant late-afternoon blue above me.

"Go, Winnie!" Cinnamon cried.

"Yeah!" Adam called.

I let go—and *whoosh*. Down I went, looping in swishy

curves, water sluicing up and into my eyes. I torpedoed into the water and shot straight to the bottom. I came up spluttering.

"Yay, Winnie!" Cinnamon and Adam cheered. Cinnamon clapped madly.

"Yay!" the unitard girl said. Her booger, by now, floated somewhere in the pool.

"Here you go," the man said, striding over and handing me a ten-dollar bill. He started off scowling, then broke into a belly laugh, which made me like him better. "You earned it."

Adam regarded me with admiration.

"I could have done it, too, you know," Cinnamon said.

"I know," I said. But the fact was, *I* did it. Me. Sometimes I was surprised by my own identity, as if I were a puzzle and life kept giving me clues to who I was. The last two days had given me two new pieces: first, that boys—and not just Lars—could conceivably like me, and second, that I could be brave when I wanted to. That was a good thing to remember, since so often I felt un-brave.

"Come, my darlings," I said to Cinnamon and Adam, holding the bill aloft as I dog-paddled to the side of the pool. "It's piña colada o'clock."

August

August was as hot as sin, and everyone on the planet was cranky. Well, everyone in the Northern Hemisphere, at least. Or whatever hemisphere we lived in. Except for maybe the people in Canada, because I think I'd heard Canada could be chilly? And Seattle. The people in Seattle might not be cranky, because in Seattle it was supposed to rain all the time. Although that much rain would be cranky-making on its own. . . .

Forget hemispheres. Forget individual states, because for all I knew there could be a freak snowstorm in north Georgia—though I found that very unlikely. If there was a freak snowstorm in north Georgia, every single Atlantan would be booking it up there as fast as their SUVs would allow. And why? Because it was the hottest August in decades.

It was so hot, my face slicked with sweat the moment I stepped outside. It was so hot, I swabbed on extra strokes of deodorant two or three times a day. My cat, Sweetie-Pie, took up permanent residence on top of the air conditioner vent, and even with the air conditioner on, the temperature in the house didn't dip below eighty. With the outside temperature in the hundreds, Dad refused to push the thermostat lower. If I nudged it down myself, he slid it back and lectured me sternly about limited resources and astronomical electricity bills.

"It's not eighty degrees in your office," I replied once (and only once) after he spelled out why suffering was good and air-conditioning was evil.

"What was that you said?" he demanded. This exchange occurred at home, so he was as cranky as I was.

"Your office, it's nice and cool there," I muttered. When Mom, Ty, and I had stopped by earlier in the week to bring Dad some papers, it had been like stepping into the refrigerated aisle of the grocery store. Or Canada.

"Winnie, I get up at six A.M. every day to put food on the table for you and your brother and sister," he said sharply. "You want to provide for the family? Go right ahead. As a matter of fact, we have a backlog of filing that needs to be done. Why don't you come to work with me tomorrow and file papers all day?"

So, yeah, I stopped complaining about the lack of AC. Didn't mean I stopped resenting it.

Ty got a heat rash, which Dad said was jock itch, which made me draw my eyebrows very dubiously together. This was Ty we were talking about! Sweet, innocent Ty. And maybe he wasn't so sweet and innocent, but he was only six. He'd be seven in a week—his birthday came just in time for the school year cutoff—but even so. Should an almost-seven-year-old get jock itch? More to the point, should an almost-seven-year-old have a *jock*?

The humidity made Sandra's blond hair puff into a fro, and she yelled at me for using the rest of her Frizz-Ease, which I hadn't touched.

But Mom. Mom was the worst. Of course the hot days got to her; they got to us all. But she blamed it on *us*, which wasn't fair. Last time I checked, I wasn't God. (Neither were Sandra or Ty, thank heavens.) But Mom got irritated by everything, and she snapped at us over nothing. She plain old wasn't fun anymore.

And then one blistering day—it was ninety-five in the shade; eighty-two in our infernally sweltering house—she lost it completely. She was fixing dinner. Her cheeks were flushed. Her hair didn't look as smooth and shiny as it normally did, and chunks kept falling in her face.

"Ty!" Mom called. "I need you to set the table!"

"No thanks," Ty yelled from the den.

I was reading a book at the granite island, and Mom looked at me irritably, as if Ty's attitude was my fault. She put down the potholder and strode to the door of the kitchen. "Not an option, bud. Get in here—it's your night!"

Ty didn't respond.

A good mother would have marched to the den and grabbed him by the ear, but Mom? She just sighed.

"Winnie, would you do it?" she said.

"Mo-o-m!" I protested. My book was at a good part.

Rachel had just discovered she had magical powers. Plus, it wasn't my turn.

"Please," she stated. It wasn't a request; it was an order, and it made me grouchy, because I wasn't the slacker here. Ty was. But I put down my book and did it, because that's me.

While I put out five plates, Mom delivered a monologue about how glad she would be when school started next month. "I was crazy not to sign Ty up for day camp," she said, closing the microwave on a dish of frozen peas and punching the ON button. "You kids are under my feet twenty-four-seven!"

"*I'm* not," I said, bristling at the "you kids" designation. And did she consider Sandra one of the "you kids"? Sandra was seventeen, for heaven's sake.

"It's over a hundred degrees outside, so it's not like I can send you out to play. I get that," Mom went on. "But I'm losing my mind! I don't think any of you understand what I go through to keep this family running!"

She checked on the tray of chicken fingers in the oven, then banged shut the door. Frozen chicken fingers out of a box, which required soooo much effort. Anyway, should a mother complain to her very own daughter about her terrible, beleaguered existence? I was hot and grumpy, too, but she didn't hear me complaining.

"And the constant whining and bickering," Mom said. "'*Ty did this,*' '*Sandra did that.*' My *god*. If I could have just one day without the three of you getting all over each other . . ."

Okay, maybe I occasionally complained. But only over stuff that was justified, like Ty sticking his feet in my face and asking if they stunk, or Sandra hogging the TV.

I folded the napkins—*folded*, because I was going that extra step—and tucked them under the plates.

"Do you wish you never had us?" I asked.

"Winnie!" Mom exclaimed. A swatch of sweaty hair fell forward onto her face. "It's hot. The house is a wreck. I haven't had a moment to myself in centuries, and I no longer own a single pair of underwear where the elastic hasn't popped out of the leg. But do I wish I never had you kids? Never."

"Well, good," I said. "Remember that." I replayed her words, realizing a beat too late that she'd snuck in a Mom-inappropriateness. "And I'd appreciate it if you kept your underwear woes to yourself."

She laughed. I felt a moment's gratification.

Then she said, "I'll tell you one thing, though. If your dad and I ever get divorced? *He* gets full custody."

My hurt must have registered on my face, because she quickly said, "I'm kidding, Winnie. I've had a long day—that's all. Your dad and I are never going to get divorced."

"I know," I muttered. I plunked down the knives, forks, and spoons without speaking, because it was the custody remark that upset me, not the bit about divorce.

Mom looked at me. I did not look at her.

"Will you call everyone to dinner, please?" she asked.

I gladly left the kitchen, because there was a stinging in my eyes that was dangerous.

"Dinner!" I yelled up the stairs to Sandra. I went to the den and poked my head in. "I set the table, so you have to clean up," I said to Ty. "Now come eat."

I found Dad in the sun porch reading the paper. "Dinner's ready," I told him.

He put down the paper and pushed up from his chair.

As we ate, Mom went over the next day's schedule. Tomorrow was Saturday, which meant chore day—not that Mom appreciated our efforts. We should revolt. We could be *so* much worse than we already were.

"Sandra, I need you to go to the Farmer's Market for me," Mom said.

Sandra groaned. "The Farmer's Market? It takes forty-five minutes to get there!"

"I've got a list. I'll give it to you in the morning. And Joel, I need you to take Ty and Winnie to get haircuts."

"I don't need a haircut," I said.

"Yes, you do," Mom said. "You're looking scraggly."

"I'm not getting my hair cut," I said. I was still growing it out for Locks of Love, which I might have explained if she wasn't being so witchy.

"Fine," she said, as if I were thwarting her on purpose. "Joel, please take Ty to Kool Kuts, and Winnie, you're going, too."

"But—"

"Get a haircut or don't, I don't care. You're *going.*"

"No problem," Dad said. He'd picked up on Mom's foul temper—who hadn't?—and was being Mister Super Jovial Man to balance it out. "We'll have fun, won't we, kids?"

"If Winnie doesn't have to get a haircut, why do I?" Ty complained.

"Because you're a boy," Mom said. "Girls can wear their hair long. Boys keep theirs short."

"That is so sexist," Sandra said, taking a bite of her chicken finger, then grimacing and putting it down. "Boys can wear their hair long if they want."

"Not when they're six—"

"Seven in seven days!" Ty interjected.

"—and not when they're living under my roof," Mom said. She remembered the microwaved peas and stood up to get them.

"I don't understand why Winnie can have long hair and not me," Ty said.

"According to Mom, because you don't have a vagina," Sandra said.

"Sandra!" Mom snapped. She clonked the dish of peas on the table.

"I do so have a bagina," Ty said. "It's called a penis."

"*Va*-gina," Sandra said. "*Va-gi-na.*"

Ty rolled his eyes. "That's what I said. Bagina."

"No vaginas at the dinner table!" Dad said.

"I can't take it," Mom said to herself. She closed her eyes and put two closed fists to her forehead.

Ty noticed the chicken fingers, which were long and finger-y instead of chunky like the good ones from Whole Foods. "Yuck!" he said. "I *hate* these yucky chicken fingers!"

Mom slammed down her hands, opened her eyes, and screamed. It was fierce and raw and not for pretend.

Sandra and I froze. Ty burst into tears. Mom glared at him, which made me hate her, even through my shock and fear. She was being so awful.

"Ellen, it's going to be okay," Dad said soothingly, but also with an edge of, *Okay, you're really losing it, hon.* "I'll take the kids to Kool Kuts. You can have the whole morning to yourself."

"I need to go for a walk," Mom said.

"Absolutely," Dad said.

"Right now, or I swear I'm going to have a breakdown."

"Go. We'll take care of everything here," Dad said. "Right, kids?"

"I'm sorry," Ty said, sniffling. "I do not hate them. I just don't like them *right now*."

"Ty, it's not your fault," I said in a steely voice. "Mom bought the wrong kind."

Dad shot me a warning glance.

"Can I have some chocolate milk?" Ty asked.

"Of course," Dad said. "Winnie, can you get Ty some chocolate milk?"

On the outside, I was a rock. On the inside, I was seething. My chair screeched on the floor as I pushed it back, and Mom winced. *Get over it*, I thought. *This is the life you picked for yourself, so buck up and deal.*

At Kool Kuts for Kids, Ty first picked the fire engine chair to sit in, then changed his mind and insisted on switching to the game chair, where he could play Nintendo while the lady cut his hair. Not that he knew how to play Nintendo. He was woefully behind in little boy skills like steering monkey-mobiles over winding rainbow racetracks.

But when the lady turned on the razor, Ty threw down the controller and clamped his arms over his head.

"I changed my mind," he said. "No haircut!"

The lady looked at Dad. Dad looked at me.

"Ty," I said. "You're already in the chair."

"No!" Ty said. "No no no no no!"

Other parents stared. Dad shifted uncomfortably. Mom usually headed up these outings, the upshot being that Dad kind of didn't know how to do it.

"Ty, you need your hair cut," he said.

"Not unless Winnie does," Ty said stubbornly.

"*Ty*," I said.

"Winnie, just get a trim," Dad said.

"What? No way!"

"If she's not, then I'm not!" Ty said. He drummed his heels against the metal base of the chair.

The haircutting lady let her wrist go limp, so that the razor dangled like a dead mouse. Her expression conveyed both contempt and impatience, which I didn't think was very good for someone who worked at a haircutting place for kids. They should only hire nice people, people who knew that not everything was perfect every second of the day, and that yes, sometimes even almost-seven-year-olds threw fits.

"Just a trim," Dad said to me. "Is it really such a big deal?"

"*Yes*," I said. "Ty's being a pain. You need to be talking to him, not me!"

"He's going through a phase," Dad said. Which was true—Ty was going stir-crazy like the rest of us.

"I'm not getting my hair cut, Dad. It's important." I tried to communicate with my eyes the whole Locks of Love thing, because I didn't want to say it out loud. Saying it out loud would taint it, given the ickiness of this situation.

Dad rubbed his temples. I felt sorry for him, but I also thought, *Hey, he's your son, not mine. And it's your wife who got you into this.*

"Then would you reason with him?" he said. "Your mother's going to kill me if I bring him home looking like a street urchin."

"Street urchin." Mom's term. Geez, she cracked the whip even when she wasn't present.

"I *want* to look like a street urchin," Ty said. "I *like* street urchins."

"Stop lying," I said. "Why don't you want to get your hair cut, for real?"

Ty glanced at Dad. Then he glanced at the haircutter lady.

I stepped closer, bending down and putting my ear way up close.

"My hair is my *friend*," he said, his breath hot. "I will *miss* it."

Oh, god. It was the fingernail thing all over again. Only the fingernail thing hadn't truly been about his fingernails . . . so what was truly bothering him now?

"Are you feeling sad about something?" I asked.

He hesitated, then nodded.

"What is it?"

"Nothing."

"*Some*thing."

He picked up the Nintendo controller. He wiggled the joystick. I straightened up in frustration.

"Sir?" the haircutter lady said to Dad. Her tone suggested that there were other children waiting, children who would be happy to get their hair cut and be given a cheap balloon.

Ty beckoned. I lowered my ear back into range.

"I don't want Mom to break into pieces," he whispered.

I was confused. He didn't want Mom to break into . . . ?

Then I got it. *Ohhhh.*

"Ty, Mom's not going to break into pieces. She's not going to break at all."

"But last night—"

"She didn't mean like that, like a plate or something. She meant that if we didn't start behaving, she'd get so overwhelmed that she'd . . ." I broke off, imagining Mom in a nuthouse. I imagined her rocking back and forth like a Weeble Wobble and never washing her hair.

"She'd what?" Ty asked.

"Never mind. Nothing's going to happen to Mom."

"How do you know?"

"Because I do. Because I'm your big sister."

"Oh."

"So . . . are you ready to get your hair cut? We're holding people up."

Once more, Ty hooked his finger to draw me close. He whispered into my ear.

"*Ty*," I said, after absorbing his request.

He made begging hands. "Please?"

I rolled my eyes and headed for the door of the salon.

"Where are you going?" Dad said.

"He's going to get his hair cut," I assured him. "Just give me a sec."

I went to our car and rooted around in the backseat until I found a grubby plastic bag with a few lonely animal cracker crumbs in it. I turned the bag inside-out over the asphalt and emptied it as best I could.

"Here," I said when I was back inside the salon.

The haircutter lady was confused. "Why are you giving me that?"

"For his hair. He wants to keep it."

She blanched. She turned to Dad, who shrugged. Then she turned to her coworker, and the look she gave her said *Why me?* as clear as day. Reluctantly she accepted the bag, pinching the uppermost edge with thumb and forefinger.

"Thank you, Winnie," Dad said as the lady shaved Ty's head and shook the clumps of brown hair into the plastic bag. "You're the best."

I raised my eyebrows. "Tell that to your wife, will you?"

For the entire next week, Ty kept his bag of hair safe and close. He placed it beside him on the sofa when he watched TV. He snuck it into his lap during dinner. He cuddled it like a teddy bear when he slept. At his birthday party, which was at the Buddy Factory, he tried to persuade Mom to buy his hair bag one of the cute buddy outfits or at least a pair of shoes.

"No, and don't ask again," Mom said, balancing a Tupperware container of cupcakes and a bag of plastic dinosaurs.

"That thing is vile," Sandra said the following afternoon during a halfhearted game of M&M Monopoly, which Ty had gotten as a present. It was still boiling hot outside, and Sandra was pissy because Bo had canceled their trip to Lake Lanier. The heat had thrown his Jeep into vapor lock—or something oil-and-gasket-y like that—and he was busy doing boy stuff to fix it.

"It really is, Ty," I said. "It's disgusting." It was a cold hard fact that hair looked far prettier when it was actually on someone's head. In a bag, it looked dull and scuzzy. It didn't help that Ty was constantly fondling the hair through the plastic, molding the individual strands into a fat mud-colored sausage.

"It's like a hair turd," Sandra said. She threw her Monopoly money into the center of the board with a gesture of finality, and I followed suit. Our game was going nowhere.

Ty opened the bag and plopped his hair turd onto the table.

"Put that thing away," Sandra said. "It smells!"

Ty lifted it to his nose. "No, it doesn't."

"Yeah-huh," Sandra said. "It smells like poop."

"Really?" Ty asked.

She grabbed it and sniffed, then tossed it back. It held its shape alarmingly well. "No, but it does smell musty. You're seven years old now. You need to throw it away."

Ty turned to me. "Does my real hair smell musty?"

I leaned toward him and inhaled. "Ugh. Yes!"

Ty giggled. He loved being musty. "Look," he said, holding the hair turd above his upper lip. "It's a mustache."

I guided his hand down to his chin. "Now it's a beard. You look like Santa Claus."

"No, you look like a pervert," Sandra said. "With musty hair."

"What's a pervert?" Ty asked.

Mom strode into the kitchen. "Hey, kids. What are you guys up to?"

"We're playing Monopoly," Ty said.

"We *were* playing Monopoly," Sandra clarified. She pushed back her chair, but didn't stand up. "I'm going to call Bo and see if his Jeep's fixed. As soon as I get enough energy."

I peered at Mom from beneath my bangs and stayed quiet, because I was still feeling hostile toward her. Or not hostile, exactly, but . . . something. In the deepest fiber of my being I knew I loved her. I mean, of course. She was my mom. But she'd been acting so strange recently, and it had twisted that easy love into a more complicated shape.

She hadn't repeated her crazy-lady screaming episode, but yesterday I'd found her in her walk-in closet, sitting with her back to the wall and her knees drawn to her chest. I'd come to ask if I could go swimming with Dinah and Cinnamon, but seeing her like that made the question fly from my brain.

"Mom?" I'd said. "Are you *hiding*?"

At least she had the decency to blush. "I just . . ."

"You just what?"

"I needed a moment to myself." There were circles under her eyes, and she was hiding in her closet. My *mother*.

"You're not having a breakdown, are you?" I said. I felt angry before she even answered.

"I don't know. Maybe," she said. Not the reassurance I was looking for.

She caught my reaction and sighed. "No, Winnie, I'm not having a breakdown. I sometimes wish I *could* have a breakdown, but I'm not constitutionally wired that way. Unfortunately."

I narrowed my eyes. She was digging herself into a hole.

"You look pale," I accused.

"My stomach's been a little queasy," she admitted.

Whoa, whoa, whoa, I thought, an insane idea blooming in my brain. Mood swings? Queasy tummies?

"Holy pickles, you're not *pregnant*, are you?"

Mom's lips twitched. " 'Holy pickles'?"

"Are you?!"

"No, Winnie, I'm not pregnant. I'm just hot and queasy and ready for summer to be over. Now—did you need something?"

That dose of weirdness had happened yesterday. Today, from my spot at the kitchen table, I studied her critically. Would we get Nice Mom or Psychotic Mom? Happy Mom or Grumpy Mom?

I hadn't seen Happy Mom in a long time.

She spotted Ty's hair turd. "Ty, put that thing back in the bag *now*," she said. "You're going to get hair everywhere."

Ty's lip trembled. I dropped my eyes.

Almost as if she'd read my thoughts—which was that she was a mean mother, and she should just move to Mexico if she hated us so much—she softened her expression and tried again.

"Sweetie, I'm sorry," she said, coming over and giving Ty a leaning-down hug. "I didn't mean to snap at you."

"You used your sharp voice," he said.

"I know. But I love you. So sorry, 'kay?"

Ty stroked his hair turd. "It is my baby," he said. "You have to be nice." His mouth did that funny sideways thing that meant he was thinking. "His name is Jimbo."

"It's a boy?" I said.

"Yes, because it has a penis."

"It *is* a penis," Sandra said under her breath.

A bit of a smile poked through my mad-at-mom mood. The hair turd—*Jimbo*—did look a bit like a penis. More like a penis than a vagina, that's for sure.

Mom put her *oh, you children* face on, but it was more pretend than real. "Well, please put Jimbo back in his crib."

"Is his crib his bag?" Ty asked.

"Yes. It's time for his nap. Babies need a lot of sleep."

"Okay," Ty said, tucking Jimbo in.

"Winnie, can I talk to you for a sec?" Mom asked.

Uh-oh. I hadn't done anything wrong—but my stomach tightened as if I had.

I followed her to the living room. She took a seat on the sofa and patted the spot beside her. I sat down, leaving a ribbon of space between us.

"Winnie, I need to tell you something," she said.

My heart beat faster. "Okay."

She started to speak, then stopped. Twin spots of color blossomed in her cheeks.

"What is it?" I said.

"I *am* pregnant," she said. She gave me a sheepish glance. "Can you believe it? Is that not the most ridiculous thing you've ever heard?"

"You're pregnant?" I repeated.

"Uh-huh. Go figure."

"You're *preg*nant."

"I'm pregnant, all right."

"Did you just find out, or did you already know?"

"Your dad and I have known for about a week."

Oh, I thought, piecing it together. *Since the screaming day.* "So you lied to me, yesterday in the closet?"

"I guess so," she said. "That wasn't good of me, was it?"

"No, it wasn't."

"But that's why I'm telling you now." She put her hand on my knee, and I looked at it. Her graceful long fingers. Her silver wedding band, because she'd always preferred silver to gold.

"It wasn't exactly a planned thing," she said slowly, checking to see if I understood.

Heat rushed to my skin as I caught her drift. *Mother. Father. Sex.*

"Uh, okay," I said.

"But you know what? I love you kids more than anything in the world. Another baby will just add to the love."

Another baby. Another baby. I knew that's what pregnant meant—duh—but the reality of it suddenly sunk in. Forget the sex, forget the lying . . . Mom was having a baby!

"I'm going to have a new brother or sister!" I exclaimed.

"And I'm going to have a new son or daughter." She smiled. "Holy pickles!"

"Do you know yet? Which it'll be?"

"I'm only eight weeks along. We won't know the baby's sex for another couple of months."

"When is he or she due?" I asked. I was pretty sure that was the right term, "due."

"Well, the baby was conceived in June, so to figure out the due date, you count nine months further."

I did the calculation. My eyebrows shot up. "His birthday will be in March, just like me!"

"Or hers, if it's a girl. Isn't that cool?"

"As long as it's not on the eleventh," I qualified.

"I'll do my best," Mom said.

"Hey, Mo-o-m," Sandra called from the kitchen. "Ty's using your hairbrush to brush his hair turd! Just FYI!"

"You mean *Jimbo*!" Ty yelled. "He was looking scraggly!"

Mom groaned. "That thing really is revolting. One good thing about babies—they're generally too little to collect hairballs."

I giggled. "Do they know? Sandra and Ty?"

She shook her head. "You're the first person I told. Other than your dad, of course."

"Oh."

She put her arm around me and drew me close. "Love you, Winnie."

"Love you, too." I rested against her for a moment, long enough to inhale her perfume, then hopped to my feet and pulled her up.

"Come on," I said. "Let's go tell them the news."

September

"THANK *GOD* YOU'RE HERE," Cinnamon said, panting. She'd jogged up the hill to the stone bench south of the junior high building, our rendezvous spot for the first day of eighth grade. She, Dinah, and I had decided to meet early so that we could stride in as a group of three. But Dinah had yet to arrive.

Cinnamon glanced around to make sure we were alone, then kicked her leg up like a Rockette. "Am I okay?" she asked.

"Huh?" I said. She was wearing brown gauchos. They were adorable and gave me serious doubts about my own wardrobe choices.

"I got my period," she said furtively. "This morning, like fifteen freaking minutes ago. Is that fair? Does God hate me?" She eyeballed me hard, then did another high-kick. I quick-checked for a telltale spot, then shook my head.

"You're good," I said.

She turned around, glancing at me from over her shoulder. "From the back?"

I gave her a thumbs-up, noting with a sinking feeling

how her white cami hit just right to reveal a sexy stripe of summer-tanned skin. “A-okay.”

She faced me and slicked her hands through her hair. She’d gotten her period for the first time only last month, so she wasn’t yet completely with the program. And periods were hard, granted. They were a pain in the butt. No, a pain in the bagina—tee hee.

Cinnamon and I both thought it was ironic that Cinnamon started her period right around the time that Mom’s period ceased. Cinnamon was excited for me about the new baby (Dinah was, too—even more so) but it drove home the point of what periods were all about. Cinnamon had turned green when she put it all together. “You mean babies eat *blood*?” she’d said. “That’s why your period goes away when you’re pregnant?”

“*No*,” I said, making a *you foolish mortal* face. Of course, the only reason I knew this was because of the crash course Mom had given me when I’d posed the same question. “The baby gets its food from the mom’s umbilical cord. Whatever Mom eats, the baby eats. The period blood forms the lining of the uterus.”

“Uh-huh,” Cinnamon said. “And the uterus . . . ?”

“Is where the baby lives. The womb.”

“Oh,” Cinnamon said.

It wasn’t often that out of the two of us, I was the more knowledgeable. But I’d had my period since seventh grade, and now I was the one with a preggo mom. So go figure.

Being the resident menstruation expert meant zilch, however, when it came to the first day of the new school year. First days scared me. They always had. Even though we were eighth graders now—and therefore the top dogs of the junior high—there was still so much pressure! Especially since today would be my first time to see Lars in three months. Eeek, eek, eekie-eek!

We'd talked on the phone since he'd gotten back from Prague, but only once. And it had been awkward.

How was Prague?

Aw, man, it was great. Prague was great.

Yeah?

Pause.

Pause.

Pause.

Crickets chirping.

Well . . . that's great!

I knew things would be better when we saw each other in person, but until the actual moment of "better" occurred, I was stuck stressing about it. And to make matters worse, my way of responding to stress—any stress—was phenomenally self-defeating.

First, I'd get totally freaked out about whatever it was: in this case, going back to school and seeing Lars again. Then I'd think way too hard about how I was going to handle it: in this case, what I was going to wear and how I'd do my hair and whether I'd go for makeup or not. Blah blah blah.

And finally I'd get disgusted with myself for being such a freak, and in my brain I'd be like, "Ah, screw it." I'd decide to not even bother, which would feel good at the time, but would leave me in the lurch when the actual scary pressure moment arrived.

As it always did.

Curse the onward marching of time! Curse Cinnamon's adorable gauchos and clingy white cami! And curse curse curse my boring jeans and "Candyland" T-shirt! The look I was going for was Girl Who Is Above It All. The look I'd achieved, I now realized, was Girl Who Belongs Back in Pre-School.

"I should have worn a panty liner," Cinnamon said, still dwelling on her female problems. "Or at least jeans, which are so much less likely to let anything show. Why oh why didn't I wear jeans?"

"Because unlike me you wanted to look cute?" I said.

"What are you talking about? You look cute." She gave me her full attention, for the first time actually registering what I was wearing. She lifted her eyebrows.

"Uh, Winnie?"

"I know. I know! Let's not dwell on it, 'kay?"

"Guys!" Dinah called, puffing up the hill in high-waisted khakis and a tucked-in pink Polo. "Hi! Omigod, you both look so great!"

Cinnamon smiled and waved. "You, too!" she called gaily. To me, she whispered, "Okay, guess what? I've decided you look *fine*. At least you're not dressed like the president of the P.T.A."

I laughed, then immediately felt guilty. But it was part of our dynamic that sometimes Cinnamon would make fun of Dinah, and sometimes I would laugh.

"Don't be mean," I told her. That, too, was part of our dynamic.

Dinah reached us, flushed and beaming. "Yay! I am so glad to see you guys!" She bounced on her heels. "I can't believe we're eighth graders. I can't *believe* it!"

"It's going to be a big year," Cinnamon said. Down by the junior high's main entrance, more and more kids poured from their parents' cars. There was squealing and hugging among the girls; among the boys, knuckle punching and high fives. From our hilltop vantage point, everything was muted and only remotely threatening.

Hello, little ant children, I said in my head. And then my stomach tightened, knowing I'd soon be joining the ranks.

"Winnie, look," Dinah said, pointing. "There's Amanda."

I slapped down her hand. What if Amanda had seen? Amanda was doing the all-black thing, I noticed, and I could see even from here that she was still in her heavy eyeliner stage.

"And oh, look, there's the lovely Gail," Cinnamon said. "Did you guys hear? She's a *model* now. She did the back-to-school issue of the Sears catalogue, whoop-di-doo."

I groaned. "Great, her ego's going to bounce right out of her head."

"I know," Cinnamon said. "But *Sears*?" She laughed. "It's hilarious when you think about it. It's like being a model for Kmart."

"What's wrong with Kmart?" Dinah asked.

Cinnamon tilted her head.

"I'm serious!" Dinah said. "I like Kmart. This shirt came from Kmart!"

Cinnamon clucked her tongue, like *the girl will never learn.*

I spotted Malena-of-the-boobs emerging from her father's Lexus, and I jerked my head to alert Cinnamon and Dinah. Malena wore a V-neck tank and a miniskirt that just barely met the dress-code requirements, and when she lifted her hand to wave at Amanda and Gail, the heads of every single male turned in gawking appreciation.

"Did you hear?" Dinah said. "She fooled around with a guy from a brand-new Disney Channel show. It was during her family's beach vacation in L.A."

"Nuh-uh," Cinnamon said.

I was skeptical, too. Seriously, a sitcom star? And how would Dinah know?

"It's true," Dinah said, reading our expressions. "Louise told me. I ran into her at Bennigan's. Malena met this guy, I think his name's Gage, on the beach in L.A. And they totally fooled around. And now Malena IMs him, like, every day, and she's hoping to be an extra on his show! *If* they need extras, which Malena thinks they will."

"What a slut," Cinnamon said.

"Cinnamon!" Dinah scolded.

"It's true! And why should girls like Gail and Malena . . . why should they be the ones who get to be in Sears catalogues and kiss movie stars? Why not us?"

"Do you want to be in the Sears catalogue?" I asked. "I thought you said it was hilarious."

"Still."

I gave her a subtle once-over. Yes, she was adorable in her gauchos and cami, but it was also true that she had a bit of tummy poking out. It was a cute little roll above her waistband. She'd had it since we first met. I didn't mind it at all. But I kind of didn't think she was model material, even for Sears.

The bell rang announcing homeroom.

"Oh, crud," Cinnamon said. "It's time."

"Yikes, yikes, yikes!" Dinah said, smoothing the pleats on her khakis. "I *really* want this to be a good year. The best year ever!"

Cinnamon lifted her chin. "Ready, you guys?"

"Ready," Dinah said.

"Winnie?"

I closed my eyes, instructing myself to be calm and confident and fabulous. And witty, if possible, but not in a show-off-y way. And kind. Always kind, which meant no more making fun of Dinah behind her back—or going along with Cinnamon when she did.

"*Win*nie?" Cinnamon repeated. She jabbed my arm with a series of impatient pokes.

I opened my eyes. "Let's do it."

I didn't see Lars and I didn't see Lars and I didn't see Lars. And why? Because he was in high school now—duh—and the high school buildings were in a different part of the campus than the junior high. It was unnerving to think of him out there in high school land, doing high school things with other high school kids. High school kids like my very own sister, Sandra, who was a senior now, which blew my mind.

Not that Sandra and Lars would move in the same circles. To us lowly eighth graders, the ninth graders were hot stuff. But to the seniors? They were nothing but lowly freshmen, just as the seventh graders, to us seasoned eighth graders, were nothing but scrawny, trembling newbies.

But the junior high and the high school shared the same cafeteria, and depending on which lunch you had, it was possible for an eighth grader and a ninth grader to cross paths. That's what I was hoping for, and that's what I got. I passed Lars as he was exiting the cafeteria, and he grinned at me and saluted. Saluted! So cute!

And oh my God, he'd only gotten more gorgeous since the beginning of the summer. His dark hair was longer, and his shoulders were broader. He was a total guy in his slouchy jeans and untucked button-down, and I had the crazy thought that I didn't know him anymore, this world-traveler-stud-boy with squinty hazel eyes. It threw me into a state of panic, no doubt because of too much nervous anticipation for this very moment.

"Off to class?" I managed, moving out of the throng of lunch traffic so we could talk.

"Nah, I've got a free," he said. He paused, too, but his eyes followed his buddies as they headed out the door. He focused back on me.

"Going to hang out on the quad?" I said. "Soak up some rays?"

"You know it."

"Nice."

He glanced at the door. "Well . . ."

"Well . . ."

"Guess I'm out of here," he said. "Enjoy the fried chicken."

"Yessir," I replied. He grinned, and my heart soared.

When I caught up with Dinah and Cinnamon, I told them they had to eat fast so we could get to the quad before Lars's free period ended. They were dear darling sweeties and complied, scarfing down their chicken in record time while I nibbled a few bites of my own and tried to think of clever conversation openers. We put away our trays, made a speedy bathroom pit stop, and headed outside.

"There he is!" Cinnamon squealed, spotting him under

a tree with his best friend Bryce and two girls I didn't recognize.

"Yes, I know," I said. "Time to hush now."

"Geez Louise, when'd he get so tall?" Dinah asked.

"Shut up shut up shut up," I said under my breath.

"Crap, Winnie, he's, like . . . gorgeous," Cinnamon said.

"Is there something about 'close your pie hole' that you don't understand?" We were within yards of him. My palms grew sweaty.

"Lars, hi!" Cinnamon called out. "Long time no see!"

Lars glanced up. A smile stretched across his face. Bryce looked up, too, as well as the two girls, who must have been sophomores or even juniors, because I really think I would have known them if they were freshmen. I would have at least seen them in the junior high halls last year.

"Sinful Cinnamon," Lars said. "What's up?"

"Winnie just told me to close my pie hole," she tattled.

"Cinnamon!" I whacked her.

Bryce laughed, and Cinnamon puffed with pleasure. Bryce, too, had gotten cuter over the summer. I could see Cinnamon taking him in.

"Sit, sit," Bryce said expansively, gesturing with his arm to show that there was enough grass for all of us.

We sat, me next to Lars and Cinnamon next to Bryce. Dinah hesitated, then plopped down on the outer edge of the circle.

"So anyway," the unknown girl closest to Lars said.

She widened her green eyes, giving him her full attention. "Prague versus Paris."

"You can't go wrong with either one," Lars said with the confidence of someone who'd been to both. He launched into an analysis of street life, cafés, and cappuccino—(cappuccino? since when did he drink cappuccino?)—and I studied the girl he was talking to. She had shiny red hair to go with her green eyes, and her skin was winter pale. She wasn't gorgeous, but there was something very . . . high-school-and-not-junior-high about her. A silver hoop glinted in her left nostril.

She must have felt me staring at her, because she turned and looked at me. *Yes*? she seemed to say with an arch of her eyebrows.

I blushed. Lars turned to look at me, too, and I wanted him to put his arm around me, to show her that I belonged. That I wasn't the interloper here.

"Have you been to Europe?" I asked. See? I was being polite. Mature. Marginally functional despite my lowly eighth-grade status.

"Me?" she said. She made it seem like a dumb question, which it wasn't. It wasn't dumb to ask someone if she'd been to Europe if Europe was what everyone was discussing. "No, I've only traveled to the Americas."

"Oh," I said. I didn't even know what that meant, "the Americas." Was she making fun of me? Or was she talking about Brazil or something?

Her friend snorted, which solved the mystery. She was making fun of me.

"I've been to Europe," Cinnamon interjected.

"No, you haven't," Dinah said.

Cinnamon laughed. "Okay, you got me. But I want to."

"Don't we all?" the friend of the girl with the nose ring said. She was Indian, with super glossy black hair, and now, because she was being nice, I wondered if I'd misinterpreted her snort. Maybe I'd also misinterpreted the redheaded girl's "Americas" remark?

I wished I could be easy and unabashed like Cinnamon. I wished I could just laugh at myself, instead of getting so anxious about everything.

Lars still wasn't treating me any differently than anyone else in the group, and I felt like I should stake my claim a little.

"Tell them about the singing barista," I said, nudging his knee with mine. "The one who only sang Britney Spears songs. The one with a really thick accent." Lars had e-mailed me about her from a cyber café. He'd typed, "*Oops! She's doing it again!*"

"Well, there was a singing barista," Lars deadpanned. He adjusted his position so that our knees didn't touch. "She had a really thick accent, because guess what? She was from Prague."

The others laughed, including Cinnamon. Dinah smiled, but her eyes, when they met mine, were uncertain. I laughed to show her it was okay, though it wasn't. Lars was the one who told me the singing barista story. He told me because he thought it was funny, so why was he turning it around so that *I* was the one who was funny—and not in a good way?

I should have left. I should have strode haughtily away with a cutting remark, or at least a withering glance to let Lars know I wasn't someone he could treat like this.

But I stayed. I stayed and forced my face muscles into appropriate expressions as Lars, Bryce, and the high school girls held their conversation, and inside, I felt hot and quivery and wrong. I fought hard to keep it under control . . . but what would happen if I didn't? If I burst into tears and said, "Lars, why are you being a jerk?"

Was this what getting older meant? Getting better and better at hiding your true emotions?

Eventually, Bryce slugged Lars's shoulder and said, "Dude, let's do it." To the girls, he said, "Physics. Dr. Teaseley."

The girl with the nose ring groaned. "I had Dr. Teaseley last year. He is so unbelievably strict."

The Indian girl said, "Didn't he used to be in the military?"

"He thinks he still is," the nose-ring girl said. "Plus, he's got the worst coffee breath. You *don't* want him getting in your face."

"Man likes his joe," Lars said.

I shot him a look, not that he noticed. *Man likes his joe?*

The guys got to their feet. The high school girls followed suit.

"See ya," Lars said to me, because apparently he was big enough to at least say good-bye.

On the inside, I was thick, black sludge. On the outside, I was nothing. Blank.

"See ya," I replied.

Mom took Ty and me to Baskin-Robbins to celebrate our first day of school, since of course I had so much to celebrate. Whoopee! Mainly I let Ty do the talking while I sat there and nudged my spoon around my cup of chocolate chip mint. Mom looked at me funny a few times, but didn't bug me about it. Maybe she understood the whole moodiness thing, being pregnant. Although in her case, it didn't affect her appetite. She finished her own two scoops of rocky road and then gestured at my cup.

"May I?" she asked.

I pushed it toward her.

"And that's a whole *'nother* thing that's different," Ty said, continuing his monologue: *Second Grade: A Whole New Ball of Wax*. "Silent. Reading. You heard it here first, folks. For an entire half hour after lunch! Right at the sleepiest time of day!"

"That doesn't sound like good planning," Mom said.

"No, it's not," Ty said. He turned to me. "Winnie, did you have silent reading when you were in second grade?"

"Huh?"

He stared at me. Then he focused back on Mom. "*And* Cody cried because Hank made fun of him for picking his nose."

Mom dragged the spoon around the ice-cream cup. "Well, Hank shouldn't have done that. But I've always told you kids not to pick your nose, and that if you do, someone's bound to notice."

"Mo-o-om, I *sneak* it," Ty said.

I took in his face, the mustache of ice cream above his upper lip. He was such a messy eater. When he was five and I was eleven, Sandra had a job here at Baskin-Robbins, and Mom used to drop the two of us off for free babysitting. This was where Sandra met Bo, actually. I had a crush on him. I used to make him show me his scooper's muscle.

Anyway, Ty was messy back then, too. Odds were he'd be messy his entire life.

Me, on the other hand. I reflected on my eleven-year-old self, so filled with importance at being at the ice-cream store without Mom, and thought, *I am not that girl anymore. I will never be that girl again.*

Ty downed his Dixie cup of water and looked at mine. "Can I have a sip? I promise I won't backwash."

Yeah, right, I thought, knowing he'd return it milky with French vanilla. But I passed it over anyway, because what did it matter?

•••

By the time we got home, it was starting to get dark. Mom stopped the car at the base of the driveway and said, "Winnie, will you please hop out and get the mail?"

"I will," Ty said, already unbuckling. He opened his door, and his voice changed pitch. "Hey, look—it's Lars!"

I snapped to attention. "What?"

Ty waved in the direction of the house. "Hi, Lars! We're here! Winnie's here!"

I saw Lars rising from one of the red chairs on our front porch, and my heart jolted into overdrive. My sweat pores, too. I scrambled out of the car.

"I'll be inside in a minute," I told Mom.

"That's fine," she said. "I wondered if something happened between you two, if that's why you've been acting poky."

"Nothing happened. I'm not poky. Bye!"

I fast-walked up the drive, sliding my palms down my jeans. Lars shifted his weight.

"Hey," he said when I reached him.

"Hey," I said. Was he mad at me? Was I mad at him?

"So . . . how'd the rest of your day go?" he asked.

"It was good. Yours?"

"Ah, you know." He did this cute thing with his eyebrows—quirky, like a puppy—that I didn't know how to interpret. Mom's Volvo zoomed up the driveway, with Ty and the mail included. When they were safely past, Lars grabbed my hand.

"C'mere," he said. I resisted for a second, then let him pull me toward him. His arms circled my waist; my knees knocked against his legs. I breathed in his smell. I felt grateful, so grateful.

Lars stepped sideways, shuffling us to the left so that his back was pressed against the house and we were as far out of sight of the front window as we could be. He lifted my chin with his fingers, making it so I had to look at him. It was hard to hold his gaze. His body was so close. *He* was so close.

"I missed you," he said.

"I missed you, too," I whispered.

He leaned in, and I stretched onto my tiptoes so our lips could meet. Which they did, again and again and again.

October

On the last Monday of October, Westminster had a teacher workday. Trinity didn't, which Ty thought was terribly unjust. He had a point: Westminster did seem to have a heck of a lot more teacher workdays than Trinity.

"Sorry, Charlie," Mom said as she picked up the crust of his Eggo to throw away. "Find your shoes. It's time to go."

"But it's not fair!" he complained, draping himself over the sofa like a sack of flour.

"Welp, life isn't fair," I said. "Never has been, never will." Which oddly enough failed to raise Ty's spirits, so to appease him, I told him I'd come be a reading volunteer with Mom. At eleven. After a lovely long bath and an episode or two of *Judge Judy*.

"For real?" he said.

"Sure," I said magnanimously. I could say "hey" to my old Trinity teachers and at the same time earn brownie points for being such a good and loving sister. Afterward, I could probably persuade Mom to take me to Pricci's for a girls' lunch.

Mom and I arrived at Mrs. Webber's room five minutes

before Reading Workshop started, and I blinked at the bright colors and construction-paper-happy bulletin boards of the second grade classroom. Squishy beanbags for the kids to flop down on: check. Class snake in a glass tank: check. Poster of a kitten clinging to a tree with the inspirational message *Just Hang In There*: check.

I felt old soaking it all in.

There was still a soft spot in my heart for that scrappy kitten, though. When I was seven, I'd loved that kitten, and I'd imagined gently lifting him from the tree branch and lowering him to firm ground. "There you go, teensy bitsy," I'd say. "Next time, don't climb so high!"

"Ellen, why don't you start with Ty," Mrs. Webber said, handing Mom the reading workbook and showing her what lesson Ty was on. Ty waved at us from his desk, which was pushed up against three other desks to make a cluster. A construction paper sign printed with the words "Crazy Crabs" hung above them from the ceiling. Other desk-clusters were labeled "Super Seahorses," "Wonderful Whales," and "Jiggling Jellyfish."

"And Winnie, I think I'll have you work with Joseph," she said. She handed me Joseph's workbook and lowered her voice. "He could really benefit from a little one-on-one. Not that he's struggling academically. Academically, he's fine. But I just love that kid. I want to give him all the TLC I can."

The three of us glanced at Joseph, who sat at the "Dapper Dolphins" cluster. He didn't notice us, but stayed bent over his spelling book, lower lip between his teeth. He wore a red knit cap, even though he was indoors. A plastic container of antibacterial gel sat on the corner of his desk.

"How's the chemo going?" Mom asked softly.

Mrs. Webber frowned and shook her head, either to mean "Not now" or "Not good." I wasn't sure which.

"So . . . do I just go over the lesson with him?" I asked.

"That's right," Mrs. Webber said. She smiled and snapped back into teacher mode. "Why don't you take him to the Commons? Find some place comfy to sit."

On an overstuffed purple sofa, I ran my finger under blocky black sentences while Joseph sounded out the words. The story was a juicy tale of suspense involving an inscrutable cat and an equally inscrutable rat. "The cat sat," he read aloud. "The cat saw a rat. The rat sat by the cat."

Oh, the joy of short A's. Might there be a bat in the cat's future? A bat wearing a hat? Who knew! That's what made it so exciting!

Joseph sighed. His skinny legs dangled from the couch in brown corduroys, and his fuzzy sweater stretched past his pale wrists. It wasn't the kind of sweater a boy would usually wear. It wasn't girly, exactly, but it also wasn't rough and tumble. It smelled nice, like laundry detergent.

"Um . . . do you want to keep going?" I asked.

He gazed up at me. His expression said, *Would you?*

I bit back a smile. He was such a little man, martyred by the cat and the rat. And it *was* a dumb story.

"Want to read something else, then?" Bookshelves lined the Commons, filled with picture books and chapter books and even big thick ones like *Harry Potter*.

"We're not allowed," he said.

"What? That's silly. Sure we are."

He looked dubious, but I felt utterly confident of my position. Maybe I wouldn't if I still went to Trinity, but I didn't. I was in junior high, and next year I'd be in high school. Joseph and I could read whatever we darn well pleased.

I strode to the shelves and pulled free a book with a bright green spine. It was *Shrek*. It wasn't the Hollywood version, but the real live story, which I guess came before the movie. I hadn't known there was a pre-movie version.

"How about this?"

Joseph quickly nodded. He was shy, which I found appealing, and it was clear he wasn't the type of boy who was a yeller and a hitter and a kicker. Another kid from Ty's class, his name was Taylor, had come home from school with Ty a week ago, and he'd dumped all of Ty's toys from their plastic bin and lobbed them at the wall. Then he called me "Whiny McTattletale" when I told him to quit. I thought that was so obnoxious.

I read to Joseph about the trials of being an ogre. By the middle of the story, Joseph had scooched close enough that our bodies were touching, and by the last page, his cheek was against my arm as he peered at the illustrations. Joseph was a skittish woodland creature, that's what went through my head, and it was my job to stay still and not scare him off. Maybe a chipmunk? Or an owl, with that fuzzy sweater of his. I thought about how he had leukemia. It made me sad.

At break time, Ty ran out to the playground with the other kids. Joseph, too, except he didn't run. He walked. Mrs. Webber waited till the room was empty, then said, "Oh, Ellen. That poor kid."

Mom put the last workbook on the stack and joined Mrs. Webber at her desk. "Is he not doing well?" she asked.

"He never complains," Mrs. Webber said. "And the other kids, they're so good. They just know that this is Joseph, and he lost his hair, and he's absent a lot. They don't make a big deal of it." She pressed her lips together. "But, no. The treatment's not working the way the doctors wanted."

"Oh, no," Mom said. "I'm so sorry."

"I know, I know." Mrs. Webber's eyes were worried. "Things could change, there's still hope, but . . ."

Mom touched her arm. I thought of Joseph, touching my arm. All the touching. All the humans.

I was proud of Mom for not saying something fakey, because that would have been wrong. I told myself, *This is what you do when there's something sad. Just touch.*

"I am such a fool," Mrs. Webber said, putting her own hand over Mom's and patting. "Do you know what I said to him yesterday? He told me he wouldn't be at school on Halloween, because he'd be with his mom. That they were spending the day together. And you know what I said? I said, 'Oh, how fun! What are you two going to do? See a movie? Go to the museum?' "

Mom clucked, but not unkindly. More like, *oh, dear.*

"What *are* they going to do?" I asked. I understood that Mrs. Webber's question had been the wrong one, but I didn't get why.

Mrs. Webber turned toward me, surprised. Had she forgotten I was there?

"I suspect they'll be at the hospital," she said. "He's due for another round of chemo, and there I was asking if he was off to the museum."

"Oh," I said. Now *I* felt dumb.

Mrs. Webber gave Mom's hand one last squeeze. "Well. Enough of my gloom and doom—and you with a brand-new baby on the way! What in heaven's name is wrong with me?"

Mom smiled. She slung her purse over her shoulder and said, "Winnie? You ready?"

I hopped off the desk I'd been sitting on. It belonged to the "Hilarious Humpbacks" cluster. The dangling sign showed a sky blue whale.

"I hope things take a turn for the better," Mom said to Mrs. Webber. "I hope Joseph and his parents get good news."

Mrs. Webber bobbed her head in a series of short, quick nods. "Oh, Ellen. I do, too."

•••

Mom dropped me off at Cinnamon's, because I ended up not wanting to go out to lunch after all. I wanted to be with my friends. I *needed* to be with my friends. I needed the reminder that most of life was happy.

Cinnamon and Dinah met me at the front door, but instead of welcoming me in, Cinnamon took me by my shoulders and turned me right back around. She and Dinah were wearing their jackets. They both smelled of "Very Irresistible," Cinnamon's favorite perfume.

"Where are we going?" I asked as they led me down the walk.

"Bryce's," Cinnamon said. She was wound up; I could tell from the spots of color on her cheeks. "Lars called, looking for you, and said people are going to Bryce's to play pool."

"Oh," I said. I'd been counting more on quality girl time, but pool with the guys would be fun. *Unless* . . .

"By 'people,' did he say who he meant?" I asked.

"No," she said.

"Is Nose-Ring Girl going to be there?"

"Ew," said Dinah. She and I shared a look. Hers was sympathetic; mine said, *Uh, yeah, that would not be good.*

"Winnie? Dinah? Chill," Cinnamon said. Her pace was brisk and determined. "If she's there, we'll ignore her. But we're going, and that's final."

Dinah and I shared another look, this one about Cinnamon's burst of attitude. Did anyone suggest not going? No. Did anyone throw out the barest *hint* of not going? No.

"*Oka-a-ay*," Dinah said.

Cinnamon glanced at her. "What?"

"What do you mean, what?" Dinah said.

"You know what I mean. Why are you acting weird?"

"Me? I'm not acting weird. You are!"

"You both are," I said.

Dinah let out a yelp of betrayal.

"Could we get a move on, please?" Cinnamon said. "I want to get there before they cue up."

"Is that so?" I said. "You suck at pool." I waggled my finger. "Something's fishy, missy. I'm keeping my eye on you."

Dinah thrust her head forward so that her actual eye was pressed against Cinnamon's arm. "Me, too," she said, giggling. "I'm keeping my eye on you." She walked hunched over and took hoppity steps to keep the position.

Cinnamon shrugged her off, but a smile flicked at the corner of her mouth. "God! You are such freaks, both of you!"

By the time we got to Bryce's, the guys—Bryce, Lars, and two other sophomores—were heavy into a game.

"Winster!" Lars called. He beckoned with his hand. "I'm kicking some serious booty. Come be my good luck charm."

Nose-Ring Girl was *not* there—happy happy joy joy—so I went over and let him pull me into a squeeze.

"Hey," he said, kissing my nose.

"Hey," I said back.

Dinah came and stood beside us, while Cinnamon took on the job of cheering for Bryce. She was feisty and high-spirited, full of "Dude!"s and high fives, and it dropped into my brain with a clunk: Cinnamon was crushing on Bryce. Cinnamon was crushing on Bryce! Of course!

By the looks of it, Bryce was totally willing to take her on. He checked to make sure she was watching before making a tricky shot, and when he sunk the stripy "nine" ball into the corner pocket, he cried, "Yes!" and gave her a supposedly spontaneous bear hug. But I knew how these things worked. That hug was planned. That hug was a move.

Oh my frickin' God. Cinnamon was going to start going out with Bryce, and we'd become a foursome: Me and Lars and Cinnamon and Bryce. And five thousand years from now, we could have a double wedding.

Only, where did that leave Dinah? I scoped out the other two pool players, checking for potential. Adam, who had curly blondish hair, already had a girlfriend, I was pretty sure. Amy something-or-other? Who played the flute?

But Dave was single—at least as far as I knew. He wasn't all that cute, but he wasn't hideous. He had bad skin, that's all. And his hair was on the greasy side. And his jeans—let's face it—came way too high on his waist. Maybe that was a good thing, though. Not the jeans, but his whole not-a-stud-muffin package, because even though it wasn't fair and I shouldn't even think it and it certainly wasn't Dinah's fault . . . well, odds were a stud muffin wouldn't be Dinah's perfect match. Someone like Dave maybe was?

After Lars won the pool game and thrust his pool stick into

the air and did a victory dance—go Lars!—the group took a break for Cokes and Doritos. Cinnamon sat on Bryce's lap, which I thought was extremely brazen, and perhaps even a bit much. But, whatever. I did a quick scoocheroo on the other sofa so that there wasn't room for Dinah beside me, forcing her to sit by Dave instead. I found Lars's hand and squeezed it.

We talked about Halloween and whether anyone was going to the school party—the consensus was "no"—and whether people were going to go trick-or-treating.

"Candy, dude," Dave said. "You think I'm going to let that wealth go to waste?"

Candy, I thought. *Very good—Dinah likes candy*. I nodded at her encouragingly, and she crinkled her eyebrows in confusion.

"You gonna steal it from some little kid like you did last year?" Adam said. He laughed, and Lars made the mistake of joining in. I elbowed him. Stealing candy from innocent children was *not* good. One point for Dave, one strike against.

"We're going trick-or-treating, right, Winnie?" Dinah said. "I love trick-or-treating."

"Um . . ." I said. I was hesitant to commit, since maybe trick-or-treating, like the school party, was passé this year. And then I scolded myself for caring.

"Better not," Cinnamon said, patting her tummy. At first I thought she was poking fun at herself, because she did have a little tub. But the way she was arching her eyebrows and giving Dinah a knowing look—an intentionally overblown knowing look—clued me in that her comment wasn't aimed at herself.

The guys laughed, and Cinnamon grinned. Dinah turned red.

"We had our fat index measured last week?" Cinnamon said. "In PE?"

Adam and Dave nodded; they'd been through it as freshmen themselves. The PE coach used these barbaric metal pincher things to squish our fat, and it was all very public and humiliating.

"Dinah scored the highest of anyone," Cinnamon said. "Didn't you, Dinah?" She said it like a tease, like something cute and funny to share with the guys, and I thought, as I'd thought so many times before, that Cinnamon was the master of underhanded digs. It was her delivery that complicated things, because her tone was joshing and friendly and *we're-all-in-this-together.* And because of that, you felt like you couldn't really blame her, or get mad, without it seeming as if you were overreacting.

But bringing up someone's fat index score was not joshing. Bringing up someone's fat index score was not friendly. And I'd promised myself that I wasn't going to do this anymore, sit silently while Cinnamon made herself look good at Dinah's expense.

I opened my mouth to speak, only no words came out,

and it was because we were at Bryce's house, that's why. And Bryce was chuckling, and so were Adam and Dave. And Dave could just forget about marrying Dinah in a fabulous triple ceremony with matching bouquets, because it wasn't going to happen. He was a jerk. Dinah was way too good for him.

Cinnamon must have read something on Dinah's face, or maybe my own, because she backed off and said, "Oh, sweetie, I didn't mean to make you sad! Who cares what your fat index is?"

Dinah looked stricken.

"I know—we'll go on an exercise plan together!" Cinnamon said. "We'll start jogging, 'kay?"

"Gonna have to jog a long way," Dave said under his breath, making Adam crack up.

"Don't be mean," Cinnamon said to Dave.

"Yeah," Bryce said, and it was hard to tell if he was adding to the joke or not. He tightened his arms around Cinnamon's waist, and Cinnamon flushed happily.

"Seriously, Dinah," she said, "you have nothing to feel bad about. It just means there's more of you to love."

Bad Cinnamon. Bad me. That's what kept repeating itself in my mind the next day. And bad Dinah, too, for not just telling Cinnamon off once and for all! Instead, Dinah cornered me in the bathroom and said, "Am I fat? I want you to tell me the truth. *Am* I?"

"No," I told her, just as I'd told her the night before on the phone, and over IM, and in response to her multi-exclamation-pointed e-mails. "No, no, no, you're not fat!"

"Well, do these pants make me *look* fat?" she pressed.

"God, Dinah, don't you have anything better to worry about?" I said. "People are dying! Babies are starving! Do you think you could maybe be a little less self-absorbed?"

She blanched. And then, because she was Dinah, she blinked and said in a chastened voice, "Babies are starving? Omigod. Where?"

It wasn't starving babies I was thinking about, though. It was Joseph with his red knit cap and fuzzy sweater. The container of antibacterial gel sitting on the corner of his desk. Yet I didn't tell Dinah that, because I didn't want to . . . I don't know, turn Joseph into a pity case? Make his disease more real by talking about it? Use the sadness in his life as a topic of conversation?

But later, alone in my bedroom, snuggled under the lovely, fluffy comforter I'd had since I was Ty's age, I felt like it was all so stupid, this business of being a human and caring what we *looked* like, for goodness sake. Although I cared, too. I knew that. And to some degree maybe physical appearance did matter, but certainly not as much as, say, being alive.

So I scooched out of bed and called Dinah. I said, "You know what? Maybe you are a little chubby. But who cares? That's just *you*."

She was quiet for a few seconds, and I got a bad, clenchy feeling inside. Had I screwed up?

Then she said, "I'm not *fat*, though."

"Not fat. Just chubby. And Cinnamon was wrong to bring it up in front of the guys."

"Cinnamon can be kind of a jerk," she said in a surprisingly forceful voice.

"Yep," I said. What else could I say?

"I don't think she *means* to be," Dinah continued. "At least, I don't think she sets out with the goal of making me feel like dirt. I think she just . . . sees the opportunity sometimes."

"And doesn't stop herself," I added. I paused, the whole of her sentence soaking in. "She makes you feel like *dirt*?"

"I think she was showing off for Bryce," she said.

"I think it worked. Did you see them today after lunch?"

Dinah snorted. Cinnamon had ditched us to play arm-tickling games with Bryce out on the quad, and I'd half-wished our vice-principal, Ms. Bolletieri, had spotted them and written them up for PDA.

"I'm going to call her and tell her she was really mean," Dinah said. "After I hang up with you, that's what I'm going to do."

Whoa. Was she really? And why did that surprise me? Was it just because I never had?

"Good for you," I said.

"Or maybe I'll e-mail her, so I'll be less likely to chicken out."

"I totally think you should," I said, suspecting that if it were me, I probably *would* chicken out—even over e-mail. Holy pickles, was I an even bigger wimp than Dinah???

"Yeah," Dinah said. " 'Cause if I let her treat me like that, then I'm part of the problem. That's what I've been thinking. And if our friendship is going to mean anything—if the three of us are going to stay friends forever, which I so so so so want—then we've got to be honest with each other, right?"

"I totally, absolutely agree."

She paused. "Can I tell *you* something?"

"Uh . . . sure." My fingers tightened on the phone.

"Sometimes . . . well . . ."

"Spit it out." My heart thumped, because I had no clue where she was headed.

"It's nothing, really. It's just that sometimes . . . your hair gets a little stringy. Like, if you haven't washed it that day."

At first I felt relieved. My hair got stringy sometimes? Duh! Especially my bangs, because they got oily from my forehead, I guess. Which was gross, but having stringy hair was far better than being a jerk. Or—truth—being fat. Not that Dinah was fat. She wasn't. But whenever I saw a truly obese person, like at the mall or at a restaurant, I couldn't help thinking that existing in such a body would be an awfully hard row to hoe.

"Winnie?" Dinah said. "Are you mad?"

"What? No, no, I'm not mad. You're right, my hair does get stringy sometimes."

And then, as the words came out of my mouth, a huge wave of shame washed over me, completely disproportionate to the situation. *My hair was stringy. Everyone knew it. Everyone saw me and thought, God, that girl should take a shower.*

"Winnie? Um . . . you sound kind of funny. Are you sure you're not mad?"

Had Dinah brought up my stringy hair to punish me? If so, she was certainly justified. I hadn't stood up for her at Bryce's. I hadn't told Cinnamon to shut up.

Maybe Dinah needed me to hurt a little, too, and that's why she said it.

"Yeah, no, I swear I'm not mad," I told her. "But I've got to go, okay? I've"—I worked up a laugh—"got to wash my hair."

But then . . . I didn't. I needed to—oh boy, did I need to. Dinah was right!—but I did not get in the shower, and I did not squeeze a dollop of Neutrogena Clarifying Shampoo into my hand, and I did not scrub and scrub until my hair was shiny and clean. What good was it for me to say all these grand things about appearance not mattering if I wasn't willing to allow appearance *not* to matter? At least for one day. At least for tomorrow, which was Halloween, and which made it all the more perfect.

I'd dress up as Ugly Girl, and I'd do it with pride. I'd dedicate it to all the Dinahs and Josephs of the world, and obese people, and kids with bad skin. I wouldn't say it out loud, but that's what I'd be doing: dedicating my ugliness to beauty within, to everyone taking a chill pill and just being *nice*, for God's sake.

Cinnamon was the first of my friends to see me that next morning. She approached me at my locker, and her expression told me without a shred of doubt that my costume was a success.

"What the *heck*?!" she said. She tried to shield me from the other kids in the hall, but I pushed her away.

"Cinnamon, stop," I said, giggling. I was sweating and nervous, but I refused to back down.

"Okay, you can *not* laugh at a time like this," she said. "Did you take crazy pills this morning? Did an anvil fall on your head, and that's why you look like this?"

Perhaps she was referring to my hair, which had gone overnight from stringy to outright lanky, and which hung in clearly defined grease-clumps. Or perhaps she meant my face, utterly unbeautified with mascara or lip gloss or my Rock Star glitter dust. Then again, it could have been my stiff and ridiculous jeans, high-waisted as all get out, or my white turtleneck with the little blue whales all over it. Which I'd tucked in, thank you very much, and which, when I dug it out of my drawer, made me marvel at how many hideous articles of clothing I actually possessed, bestowed upon me by relatives and family friends and plain bad judgment.

Pulling on the whale shirt made me think of "Wonderful Whales" and "Hilarious Humpbacks," which made me think of Joseph. Which was good, because otherwise I might have abandoned my plan. It was remarkably hard to look bad on purpose, I discovered. But I lifted my chin and added a gold lamé belt with a clasp in the shape of a heart. (God only knew how I'd ended up with that gem.) I finished the look with a hat. It was jaunty. It was plaid. Enough said.

"I'm Ugly Girl," I informed Cinnamon, who was still gaping at me.

"Yes. Yes, you are. You do not see me arguing. But *why*?"

"For Halloween," I said. For my protest to count, I couldn't explain it further than that.

Cinnamon shook her head. "No. Uh-uh. Go change."

"I'm not going to change," I said.

Dinah hurried up to us, looking quite pretty in a pink sweater that brought out the rosiness of her cheeks. "Guys, I ran into Louise, and she said I had to go find you, Winnie, because—" She broke off, taking in my fashion statement.

"Because why?" I said.

"Er . . . she said you'd gone 'round the bend. Which I didn't understand . . . but now I do?" She gave a pained smile that said, *Oh, God, Winnie, what have you done?*

"She's Ugly Girl," Cinnamon explained with narrowed eyes. "Only she's going to march right into the bathroom and change, because she's not allowed to wear a costume to school."

"It's not a costume," I said.

"Oh yes it is!"

Two seventh graders walked by, being totally un-subtle as they gawked at me.

"See, I told you!" said one of them to the other.

"Leave!" Cinnamon said to them, clapping her hands and making them jump. "Show's over! Nothing here to see!"

"Does this have something to do with . . . what we talked about last night?" Dinah asked me.

Cinnamon looked from her to me. "Oh. My. *God*."

"What?" I said. Had she figured it out? Did I want her to figure it out?

"You're trying to prove some point about what a bitch I am for making Dinah feel bad, aren't you? Although how being Ugly Girl is supposed to do that is beyond me!"

I turned to Dinah. "You told her?"

"I never said you were a . . . *bitch*," Dinah said. She whispered the last word. It might have been the first time in her life she'd ever said it.

"But . . . you *were* being a jerk," I said. The words came out of my mouth. They did. I stood a little taller.

"Please, I'm begging you," Cinnamon said to me, making praying hands. "I've learned my lesson! I will be a better person from now on! I will feed the hungry and clothe the poor—just for God's sake do something about your hair!"

I got the giggles.

"You take one arm, I'll take the other," Cinnamon instructed Dinah.

"What? No!"

They didn't listen. They dragged me to the bathroom, where Cinnamon tugged off my hat and threw it in the trash.

"Hey!"

"We need to get her head under the faucet," Cinnamon said. "I know hand soap's not the best shampoo, but it's better than nothing."

"I've got a brush in my backpack," Dinah said.

They faced me.

"Now," Cinnamon said firmly. "Are we doing this the hard way or the easy way?"

They were deadly serious, that much was clear. And my bangs truly were greasy beyond belief. The bathroom mirror didn't lie.

"Fine," I said. "But the outfit stays."

"Oh no it doesn't," Cinnamon said. "We can go to lost and found. There has to be something you can change into."

"Deal with it, Cin-Cin," I said, and the beautiful thing was, I meant it. "I'm keeping the whales."

November

"Winnie, your mom has a pooch," Cinnamon said. It was after lunch, and we were heading from the parking lot to the junior high building. Mom had just delivered my history paper on the Emancipation Proclamation, which I'd left at home even though today was its due date.

"Never again," Mom had said, handing it to me with a frown.

"I know, I know," I'd replied. "Thank you *so* much!" I never intended to leave my history papers at home—or my science reports or math homework or source materials for English—but sometimes it just happened. Well, okay, often. Often it just happened. And every time, Mom would bring it to me, whatever it was. And every time, she said *never again*.

I loved my mom. She was the best.

"It's not a pooch," I said to Cinnamon. "It's a bump."

"It's not a bump. It's a baby!" Dinah said.

"Really?" Cinnamon said, laying it on thick. "You mean she's not just becoming a porker? Oh, thank God!"

"Actually, she *is* becoming a porker," I said. "The lady likes her doughnuts, I tell you."

Dinah shoved me. "Don't be mean."

"I'm not being mean! Who's being mean? Mom sends Dad out for Krispy Kremes practically every night, but do you see me complaining?"

"No, we do not," Cinnamon said.

"That's right. I love the Krispy Kreme."

Dinah giggled. "I love the" was our new catchphrase, stolen from Bryce, who at a party over the weekend had announced that he "loved the cashew." He'd popped a handful into his mouth, smacked his lips, and said it just like that: "Man, I love the cashew."

"Don't you be making fun of my Brycie," Cinnamon threatened.

We got to the junior high, and I sat on a stone bench outside the building. "I'm not! I'm not! Geez, why is everyone getting all over me today?"

"'*My Brycie*,'" Dinah repeated. She dropped down next to me. "Did you hear that? She called him 'My Brycie.'"

"I know. She loves the Brycie."

Cinnamon smacked me.

"Hey!" I protested. It wasn't as if I were spilling some great secret, after all. Cinnamon and Bryce hung out almost every day after lunch, and they usually spent at least one weekend night together, too. They didn't spend their time just talking, either. In terms of fooling around, they'd already gone farther than Lars and I had. It was obvious that Cinnamon loved the Brycie . . . but did the Brycie love her? They'd only been going out for three weeks. How could she be sure after such a short time?

"So when does your mom have her ultrasound?" Dinah asked. Dinah couldn't wait to find out whether Mom was having a girl or a boy. Neither could I.

"November seventeenth, two days after Becca's bat mitzvah," I said.

"Ooo, goodie," Dinah said. "I can't wait!"

"I still haven't gotten my invitation," Cinnamon said darkly, meaning to Becca's bat mitzvah, not Mom's ultrasound. "You have and Winnie has and even Bryce has. Why haven't I?"

"Dude," I said. "The fact that Becca invited Bryce means that of course she invited you. So chill." My invitation had come in the mail on Friday, and it was like a wedding invitation, it was so fancy. Creamy linen paper, swirly lettering, Becca's name embossed in gold. Lars received his the next day, and he was bewildered until I told him who Becca was: a girl in my grade who I wasn't really friends with, but who was inviting every single person in our class to her bat mitzvah, plus extras. I explained to Lars that Becca was inviting him as my date.

"Huh," he'd said. He didn't seem convinced that this was a good thing.

"You'll need to get her a gift," I told him, plucking the invitation from his hand and putting it on the counter. I twined my fingers through his and pressed against him.

"I will?"

"Uh-huh. It's to celebrate Becca's thirteenth birthday. That's what a bat mitzvah is."

"Why is she just now turning thirteen? Did she skip a grade?"

"Becca?" I said, lifting my eyebrows. One of the few Becca memories I had involved Becca asking me during history if Colorado was a country or a state. "Uh, no. She went to kindergarten in Alabama and the cutoff date was later, or something like that. But there'll be dancing, and probably a chocolate fountain, and it'll be absolutely fabulous. So stop making that face!"

"I've never been to a bat mitzvah before," Cinnamon said now. She squished in beside us on the bench.

"Me, neither," Dinah said. "Think it'll be like *My Super Sweet Sixteen*?"

"It will, it totally will," I told them. Louise had gotten the scoop from Becca during PE—Louise was very good that way—then passed it onto me. "Becca's inviting everyone in our entire class, plus the kids from her Hebrew school, plus at least two gorgeous freshmen guys who happen to be dating eighth grade girls."

"Nudge nudge, wink wink," Cinnamon said. The bell rang, signaling the end of our free period. "Well, kids . . ."

"Yep, it's that time," Dinah said, rising to her feet. A girl with thick bangs and glasses scuttled by, cutting across from the high school, and Dinah called, "Hi, Shannon!"

Shannon looked startled, as she always did. "Hi," she said. She hugged her geometry book to her chest—she took freshman math even though she was an eighth grader—and kept going.

"Think Shannon's invited?" Cinnamon said in a low voice.

I giggled, although I didn't know why. It wasn't a nice thing to giggle about.

"*Yes*," Dinah said defensively. She was always one for the underdogs. "If Louise really is inviting everyone, then yes."

Cinnamon pressed her hands to her thighs and stood up. "Whatev. I'm not worried about Shannon; I'm worried about me. Seriously—what if my invitation *doesn't* come?"

"Relax," I told her. "It will."

It did, and together the three of us went to the mall to buy dresses for "the biggest social event of the season." That's what everyone was calling it (I think Louise was the first), and anticipation buzzed like hummingbirds through the junior high. The girls were more excited than the boys, because we got to wear real, live prom-dress-style-dresses, but the guys were excited, too—especially after they heard there'd be food, and lots of it. There weren't a whole lot of Jewish people at Westminster, but Alex Plotkin had been to a family friend's bar mitzvah (the boy equivlaent of a bat mitzvah), and he regaled us with stories of DJs and prizes and a whole room dedicated to dessert.

"Every kind of candy imaginable," he said. "M&Ms in huge bowls. Snickers in huge bowls. Reese's Cups in huge bowls—and not just the normal Reese's Cups, but the white chocolate ones, too!"

Saturday the fifteenth finally came, and Mom dropped me, Dinah, and Cinnamon off at the Ahavath Achim Synagogue at eleven in the morning. First came the ceremony part of the bat mitzvah, and then, that evening, the party. "It's called paying your dues," Sandra said, as if she were a bat mitzvah expert. "They stick you with religion and *then* let you have your fun."

I didn't mind the ceremony, though. The synagogue looked beautiful, all lit with candles and drapey, ornate fabrics, and Becca seemed surprisingly knowledgeable and in control up there in front of us all. She was the one who ran the service, which gave me thrills of sympathetic nervousness. It was kind of like church, with lots of singing and different people standing up to say prayers and stuff, but Becca was the one who announced each segment and told what it was.

Then it was time for her Torah reading, and one of Becca's aunts or second cousins or grandmother's nieces—I never got it straight—leaned over and said, "This is good, girls. We're in the home stretch."

"Is she going to read it in Hebrew?" Dinah whispered.

"She is," the relative said. "Oh, I remember my own bat mitzvah, how scared I was!"

I was the one seated closest to her, and she took my hand and squeezed it tightly.

Becca cleared her throat and stepped behind the lectern, where a massive Torah lay open before her. She wore a pale blue sweater set and a brown wool skirt, very ladylike, and I flashed on the incongruous image of her at school last week, smiling wide with something chunky stuck in her braces.

Ancient syllables tumbled from Becca's tongue, rounded, thick, and with a random throat-clearing sound thrown in for good measure. The words sounded mysterious and beautiful. Becca, during those moments, was *more* than Becca, and I found myself wishing I were Jewish . . . although even as I wished it, I knew I'd never do anything to make it happen. I loved our Christmas crèche with its teensy baby Jesus, which Mom would get out as soon as December first rolled around. I was Christian, not Jewish. And that was cool, too.

When Becca finished the reading, she gave a short speech about it. "My section is from Genesis," she said. "It's the story of Sarah, wife of Abraham, who was told by an angel that she would give birth to a baby boy when she was ninety years old."

"I know that story!" I whispered.

"Duh," Cinnamon said. "The Torah's pretty much the same as the Old Testament, remember?"

"Oh," I said. I hadn't remembered.

Becca talked about promises and new beginnings and cute little babies, and Dinah patted my leg to mean, *You! You're going to have a baby!*

Well, not me, but Mom, which was close enough. I did

love that this was what Becca's reading was about, though. Becca's relative had explained to us that the readings were assigned based on the Hebrew calendar, and that the rule in Hebrew School was "You get what you get, and you don't throw a fit." A kid's assigned section might be full of action, like Noah's Ark, or it might be archaic Hebrew law, like what to do if your oxen has "relations" with someone else's oxen. Ooo, I pitied the kid who had to make a speech about that.

But babies and miracles and the promise of new life? It was lovely. It made me feel special. It's possible Mom wouldn't appreciate being compared to ninety-year-old Sarah, but face it: Mom was old! And she was pregnant. And I was going to have a new baby brother or sister.

(But hopefully—secretly!—a sister? Please please please? I wanted to be a big sister to a new little girl-person, just like Sandra was a big sister to me. Only I'd be nicer. And if we had a third girl, Ty could retain his status as "only boy." But if we had a boy . . . well, obviously I'd deal.)

Becca finished her speech, and the president of the temple gave her a pair of candlesticks and her very own Torah. And then the ceremony was over. I sighed in satisfaction. My only regret was that Lars hadn't gotten to experience it, because I was sure he'd have appreciated it. But he'd opted out, along with Bryce. They *weren't* paying their dues—though they fully planned to participate in the evening festivities.

I felt a pang, there in the synagogue, as everyone stood up

and burst into animated chatter. A voice whispered in my head, *Are you sure he would have appreciated it? Are you sure he's the person you think he is, and that you're not just making that up in your head?*

I pushed those thoughts away. Yes, Lars disappointed me sometimes. So? The key word was "sometimes," like that day on the quad with Nose-Ring Girl, when he made me look stupid so she would laugh. Or when he paid more attention to Bryce than to me. Or how he seemed to think kissing would make everything better, no matter the problem.

Faith, I told myself. *Hope. The promise of new life.*

In conclusion?

Get over it.

The party. Ah, the party. There *was* a DJ, and there *was* a chocolate fountain, and there were stacks of presents and a birdcage full of envelopes, all for Becca.

"Why a birdcage?" Dinah asked, and yet another friendly relative explained that the envelopes most likely held cash or checks, and that keeping track of all that money was a bit much to expect a thirteen-year-old to do. Hence the birdcage.

Becca herself was paraded out on a litter supported by four poles, each of which rested on the shoulders of a Chippendale look-alike costumed in full Egyptian regalia. Becca was decked out in a full-length ivory evening gown, which had nothing to do with Egypt as far as I could tell. Then again, a bat mitzvah had nothing to do with Egypt, either.

"It *is* like *My Super Sweet Sixteen*!" Dinah squealed. "Omigod!"

"'Omigod' is right," Cinnamon muttered. "She so stole the whole Egyptian theme idea. Has she no shame?" But her eyes were bright as she took it all in.

Becca gave a queenly wave and descended from her hand-carried throne. "Thank you all for being here!" she said into a mic at the front of the rented-out ballroom. "Um . . . there's a video booth in the back"—she pointed—"and over there, there's a slot machine and a tattoo station—"

"Temporary!" Becca's mother called out. Her hair was poofy, and sparkly earrings caught the light like miniature disco balls. "*Temporary* tattoos, don't worry!"

Everyone laughed—well, at least the grown-ups—and Becca rolled her eyes.

"And if you want to get henna-ed, you can do that, too," she said. The mic screeched. She blinked. "So, um . . . have fun!"

The DJ swooped down to take the mic as everyone clapped. "Let's start things off with a game of Coke and Pepsi, what do you say? Everyone find a partner!"

"Coke and Pepsi?" Dinah said. "What's that?"

"I have no idea," I said. I'd never been to a party remotely like this. I felt like I was in Hollywood.

"Partners, partners!" the DJ called. His suit was electric blue, and his hair was as poofy as Mrs. Rubenstein's. I revised my "Hollywood" thought, deciding that the party was more like being in . . . gosh, I didn't know. Vegas?

Cinnamon grabbed my arm. "There they are!" she cried, dragging me across the room. She'd spotted Bryce and Lars by the door, both in suits that were mercifully not electric blue. So handsome!

"What about me?" Dinah wailed. "Who's going to be my partner?"

"Find someone!" Cinnamon called over her shoulder.

Lars greeted me with a squeeze. "This is nutso," he whispered in my ear.

I grinned. "I know, don't you love it?"

Bryce gave Cinnamon a full-on, lip-locked, tongue-action kiss, and I had to physically tug her away from him.

"God, you guys," I said. There were grandparents here!

"Now line up," the DJ commanded, his voice booming over the sound system. " 'Cokes' on the right; 'Pepsis' on the left. Don't keep me waiting, kids!"

In the middle of the ballroom, two long lines formed. The girls all went to one side—the Coke side—and the boys to the other.

"Guess we're Pepsis," Bryce said, somehow managing to make it sound dirty.

We joined our respective lines, standing opposite of each other. Cinnamon blew kisses at Bryce.

"Is everyone ready?" the DJ asked.

"No!" Bryce yelled.

A bunch of kids laughed.

"I said, is everyone ready?" the DJ asked again.

"No!" dozens of kids yelled.

"All right, then!" the DJ said. "*Coke*!"

All of a sudden, a mass exodus took place. The girls dashed to the other side in a flurry of giggles and squeals, and one girl slipped and fell. She was sock-footed, I noticed. Where were her shoes?

"Run!" Cinnamon said. So I did. We ran to our long-lost Pepsi partners, who pulled us into the fold with high fives and "yeah!"s. Bryce pinched Cinnamon's butt, and she giggled and swatted him.

"Girl in pink, you're out!" the DJ said to the sock-footed girl, who was the last to reach the Pepsi side. "Find your partner and clear the floor!"

"Aw, man!" complained a guy in a brown suit. He and the girl in pink joined the sidelines of aunts, uncles, and grandparents, who clapped politely.

Then the rest of us girls, the un-loser girls, trooped back to our other side and reformed our line. This time, the DJ called, "Pepsi!" Lars easily outpaced the other guys, and we stayed safe. So did Bryce and Cinnamon. I searched for Dinah and found her midway down the line with a gangly guy from Louise's Hebrew School.

"Good job!" I called, since they, too, remained in the game. Dinah waved, looking embarrassed but pleased.

The game continued, with the DJ mixing things up and belting out "Sprite," "Mountain Dew," and, in a surprise twist, even "San Pellegrino." The Jewish kids seemed to know exactly what to do, but I had to watch and figure it out. "San Pellegrino," for example, meant we weren't supposed to do *anything*, and the kids who dashed out on autopilot got a "Bzzzzz" and a thumb-jerk from the DJ. That one worked to my advantage, but "Orange Crush" meant the girls were supposed to skip to the other side, and I ended up being the last to arrive.

"Sorry," I said to Lars as we took the walk of shame to the patter of light applause. I was sweaty and hot.

"No worries," Lars said. He put his hand on my head and ruffled me up, so that I had to duck out of his grasp. "Got to work on those skipping skills, though."

Cinnamon and Bryce went out on a no-warning "Coke" call that caught almost everyone by surprise. Dinah and her mystery boy held on for two more rounds, then went out on "Mountain Dew." They were supposed to switch places, but Mystery Boy just wasn't quick enough. On the side, he and Dinah shook hands and parted. Dinah trotted over and joined me and Lars.

Soon there were only two couples remaining: two girls and two boys. One of the girls was Malena of the Boobs, whom the guys on the sidelines were having quite a fine time watching. (Cinnamon had to swat Bryce again for making a rude remark.)

The other girl, astonishingly, was Shannon. Shannon, who took ninth grade math, and who obviously *was* included on Louise's guest list, even though she was a social outcast. She looked painfully out of place in this glitzy ballroom, wearing a burgundy shirtdress and wool socks. Yes, wool socks. I checked out the ever-growing pile of shoes over by one of the tables, and sure enough, there among the heels and loafers was a single pair of beat-up leather hiking boots.

"Yessir, this is high drama!" the DJ cried. "Only two couples left. Who will take the prize?"

Malena looked bored, but she had to care a little, or she wouldn't have made it this far in the game. Her partner, Chip, was a guy in our grade I felt intimidated by. He was a jock, and he wasn't very nice. At least, not to me. Shannon's partner was another guy from Becca's Hebrew school. He was short and had dark hair. His cheeks were ruddy.

"Your guy was cuter," I said, leaning in toward Dinah.

She nodded. "I know."

"All righty then. Are we ready?" the DJ inquired.

"No!" yelled the crowd, led by Bryce.

"Root-beer Float!" the DJ cried.

Shannon's partner sprinted across the room, and Chip, after a moment's hesitation, followed suit. Once there, Shannon hopped with grim determination onto her partner's back, piggyback style.

"Get on! Get on!" Chip said to Malena.

"In my dress?" Malena said. "I don't think so!"

Shannon and her partner were already halfway back to the other side.

"Just do it!" Chip said.

"No way!"

"We have our winners!" the DJ crowed. "Come on up, kids, and claim your prize!"

Shannon never cracked a smile: not when her partner played to the crowd by bowing and saying "Thank you, thank you," not when the DJ raised her hand in triumph, not when she received her oversized inflatable saxophone.

"How did she know what 'Root-beer Float' was?" Dinah asked. Most of the other kids, including Cinnamon and the guys, had already dispersed. "Is she Jewish?"

"I have no idea," I said. "But she must be, huh?"

"Or else she's been to lots of bat mitzvahs."

I watched as Shannon walked away from the stage and offered her saxophone to a little girl with pigtails. The girl beamed. Shannon stayed dour. I thought about Becca and how weird it was that she'd invited this huge crowd to her party, many of whom were practically strangers. I thought how weird it was that you could go to school with someone for days and weeks and months and still not ever know them.

By all accounts Becca's party was a grand success. Yes, Bryce made fun of it, and yes, he said, "Let's not and say we did" when the DJ called all the kids forward for a rousing game of "Huggy Bear."

"But I want to play 'Huggy Bear'!" Cinnamon whined. She didn't even know what 'Huggy Bear' was. How could she? But that was how she and Bryce operated. They were a bickering sort of couple, constantly needling each other. And then they'd go off and fool around, which in fact they did in the coat closet of the hotel ballroom. The coat closet! I was so shocked, I didn't know how to respond.

It made me appreciate Lars, despite the fact that he also refused to play "Huggy Bear." He said, "Let's make a video instead. Let's do the flying carpet one." We took our places on the floor in front of the monitor, and the grown-up in charge called out directions like, "Lean to the left! Now to the right! Hold on tight, you're going through a wind tunnel!" We ended up with an awesome souvenir DVD of the two of us swooping through the night sky on a magic carpet, thanks to the miracle of digital photography. I knew I would keep it forever.

Dinah showed off her dance moves with her Hip-Hop Club buddy, Vanita, and Lars was like, "Wow, she's good."

"Tell me about it," I said proudly.

We ate popcorn, popped right in front of us in an old-fashioned kettle corn tub.

We cruised the dessert table and stuffed ourselves with chocolate mousse and gummy bears and sundaes from the sundae bar.

Lars played the slot machine.

I got a henna tattoo, along with Louise, who'd been acting all night like she was much better friends with Becca than she was.

And at the end of the night, I told Becca I had a really, really good time, and Lars nodded and said, "Yeah. Thanks."

See? I told myself. *He's a good guy.*

I knew people would be talking about Becca's party for days, possibly for the rest of time. But I missed Monday's post-op, because on Monday, Mom had her ultrasound appointment. Sandra and I hadn't gotten to go the time she was pregnant with Ty, so this time we were like, "You *better* let us." Of course Ty wanted to come, too, and even Dad took the morning off from work.

As the five of us filed into a cramped office in the Women's Clinic, I drummed my fingers against my jeans. My stomach was jumping. Why was my stomach jumping?

Mom climbed onto a padded table, lay back, and held Dad's hand as the ultrasound technician squirted clear ooze onto her belly.

"How are you doing, Ellen?" Dad asked. "You doing all right?"

"Aside from the fact that my bladder's about to burst?" Mom said.

"Mo-o-m," I said. I was aware of how much water she'd been told to drink prior to the exam, and yes, I sympathized. Still, she *so* didn't need to say "bladder" in front of God and the whole world.

"This won't take long, and then you can go to the bathroom," the ultrasound technician said.

Ty giggled. Sandra flicked his head with her finger.

The ultrasound technician placed a wand type of thing on Mom's belly. On a TV screen, a black and white image appeared, but not of anything I could recognize. There were sounds, too. *Waw-waw-waw-waw-waw*, that's what it sounded like.

"That's the baby's heartbeat you're hearing," the ultrasound technician said.

"So cool," Sandra said.

The technician moved the wand. In a reverent voice, though surely she'd done this thousands of times before, she said, "And there's the baby."

I gazed at the screen. At first I couldn't make out what I was seeing—and then I could. There was the baby's head, and the baby's curled-up body. Little fingers, clear as day. Little toes. A *baby*, a tiny living creature, just as amazing as Sarah's miracle baby, prophesied by the angel. A baby who one day would cry and laugh and smile and frown. Who would kiss and be kissed. Who would have happy days and sad says, but hopefully more that were happy.

Something huge swelled within me and made tears rush to my eyes. Sandra got teary, too. And of course Dad, because he was the biggest softie of us all. He squeezed Mom's hand in a series of pulses—I could see his muscles flexing—until Mom said, "Sweetie, you're cutting off my circulation."

"Sorry, sorry!" he said.

"Is it a boy?" Ty asked.

The technician looked at Mom. "Do we want to know?"

Mom nodded. Her eyes were shiny, too.

"Well, let's see," the technician said. She moved the wand. She peered at the screen.

"Is it?" Ty said.

I held my breath. I would be fine with it either way, I decided. I really would.

"It's a girl," the technician announced. "You're going to have a baby sister."

"Aw, *man*," Ty said, his tone the same as if Mom had announced we were having Brussels sprouts for dinner.

"A girl," Dad said. He smiled at Mom.

"How lovely," Mom said, blinking. She let go of Dad's hand and pulled Ty toward her. "And you, my darlingest darling, will make a wonderful big brother."

He submitted to the hug, then pulled away and pointed at the screen. "Look! She's waving!"

Sandra snorted. "She's a fetus. She's not waving."

But on the screen, the baby's hand was indeed moving. Five teensy-tiny fingers, undulating like seaweed.

"I think she is," I said. I looped my arm around Ty, and he bonged against me like a pinball. "Anyway, who says fetuses can't wave?"

"Hi, baby," Ty said, waving back at the computer image. "Sandra, say 'hi' to the baby!"

Sandra groaned. "Hi to the baby," she said.

"Your turn," Ty said to me.

"Hi, baby," I said happily. I looked from the computer to Mom's rounded belly. "Hey there, little sis."

December

THUS BEGAN THE NAME GAME. Now that we knew we were having a little girl, the question became, "What will we call her?"

Dad was his maddening, aren't-I-a-riot self, suggesting impossible names like "Lucretia," "Fifi," or "Mr. Tooth Decay."

"*Da-a-ad*," Ty groaned. "She's a *girl*."

"Okay, Mrs. Tooth Decay," Dad suggested.

"She's not married," I pointed out. Although a girl in my class had just gotten a new sister from Ecuador, and on the baby's passport, it said the baby was married. Stacy said it was just one more thing her parents had to undo in terms of paperwork, but we all thought it was funny. A four-month-old, already married.

"How about Esme?" Sandra said.

"Ew," I said.

"I kind of like Esme," Mom said from the counter, where she was peeling a peach.

"I vote 'no' on Esme," Dad said. "How about Peach?"

"Yeah!" Ty said.

"I vote 'no' on Peach," Mom said.

"Why not?" Dad said. "It's cute. Peach. And if movie stars can name their babies 'Apple' or 'Pilot Inspektor' or 'Chutney,' then why can't we name ours 'Peach'?"

"Because we're not movie stars, thank goodness," said Mom. She opened the freezer and drew out a bag of frozen blueberries.

"How about Mary, like Jesus's mom?" Ty said. We'd put out our crèche the night before, so Mary was on his mind.

"Mary Perry?" I said. "Blech!"

"Well then how about Terri?" Dad said. "Or Kerri? Or Terri-Kerri?"

"Terri-Kerri Perry?" I said.

"Loud noise coming," Mom warned. She pressed down on the plastic top of the Magic Bullet, which was an early Christmas present from Dad's parents, and a violent whirring prevented further discussion. The Magic Bullet was a high-powered drink blender, and when Mom first opened it, she laughed. But now she loved it. She made smoothies with it every morning because it was such an easy way to get vitamins and nutrients. Vitamins and nutrients were very important to her these days.

The whirring stopped, and Mom poured and distributed our blueberry smoothies.

"I know! Blueberry!" Dad said. "Blueberry Perry. It's perfect!"

"Enough," Sandra told him. "If you're not going to say something productive, don't say anything at all." She took a swig of smoothie, then bared her teeth, knowing they'd be flecked with blueberry skin. We'd quickly learned that of all the fruits, blueberries were the most tooth-sticky-ish.

Ty giggled.

Mom said, "Sandra, must you?"

Dad, of course, insisted on bringing the conversation back to him. "I can't believe you called me unproductive. Just because you don't like every suggestion I make, that doesn't mean it's not productive. It's called brainstorming!"

"No, it's called a waste of time," Sandra said. "And some of us don't have the time to waste."

"Hey!" Dad protested.

We regarded him, all four of us. He was alone in the wilderness on this one.

Although to be honest, the truth of Sandra's proclamation went beyond Dad's particular brand of annoyingness. The Name Game was fun, but normal life galloped along as well, and we all had plenty else on our minds.

For Sandra, it was the stress of college applications, which were due in one week. Technically, the deadlines weren't until the middle of January, but Westminster required the seniors to turn in their completed forms before they went on break. Then Westminster would mail them out, after making sure that all the i's were dotted and the t's were crossed. This wasn't normal procedure, I knew. This was hardcore private prep-school procedure, and it had Sandra pulling her hair out.

Ty had a lot on his plate, too. He was the copresident of

a new club at school called the Bad Scary Dry Cleaners, and he had a lot of responsibilities, like chasing girls around the playground.

"What do you do if you catch them?" I asked when he first told me about this. I vaguely remembered a similar chasing game from last year, when the first grade girls tried to kiss the first grade boys.

"Nothing," Ty said. "Then they chase *us*, and we scream, like this." He emitted a sonar-high squeal. "Did I sound like a girl?"

"No, you sounded like a boy, because you are a boy." He was always trying to "scream like a girl" these days. I was determined to ride it out. "Why do you call yourselves the Bad Scary Dry Cleaners?"

"Because we run around and scare people."

"But why the Dry Cleaners?"

"I don't know. And that might not be it, but something like that." He exhaled loudly. "You can see why it is a lot on my plate."

Well, sure. 'Course I could.

Mom and Dad were wrapped up in boring Mom and Dad stuff, that's what kept them busy, and for me, there was the great and daunting task of completing my Christmas list. By that, I meant making my list of what I wanted to get for everyone, not what I wanted for myself.

Cinnamon and Dinah were easy: I was going to get them both "Life Is Good" shirts. So cute. I'd picked stuff out for

Mom, Dad, and Sandra as well; as for Ty, his present was already bought and wrapped. It was an iridescent green lizard stuffed with rice or beans or something. Whatever it was, it made it super heavy. I imagined Ty draping the lizard over his shoulders and walking around with it. I knew he'd get a kick of it.

But Lars . . . ack. What to get for Lars? It needed to be special and romantic and awesome, but not *too* special and romantic and awesome. Not overly so. The point was for him to love it, not for him to get tense and think, you know, that I thought we were more than we were.

Whatever that was.

And in addition to Christmas pressure, there was the question of me and Lars that kept my brain spinning. There was something wrong between us, much as I hated to admit it. Or maybe not wrong, but . . . not right. What was it?

The Lars who lived in my brain had such potential. He was the perfect boyfriend: funny and sweet and charming and kind. And the real Lars had all that inside of him, too, I knew he did. But sometimes it got stuck, somehow.

Or maybe the problem was me, and the fact that I worried about it too much. Why couldn't I just open my heart to him and love him the way he was?

Love. Eeek. Big scary word.

I would never say that word to Lars. Cinnamon said the L-word to Bryce, after they fooled around in her bedroom one day when her dad was late getting home from work.

But he didn't say it back. Her explanation was that boys take longer with that stuff, but I didn't know. I worried for her.

However, I had a date with Lars tonight—he was coming over to watch a movie—and I was determined to let go of my tightness and just have fun. That was the best way to make things work between us.

To do that, I needed to be my most relaxed, and to be my most relaxed, I needed to feel confident and beautiful and all that. Which called for a nice, long bubble bath. And a book! A lovely, delicious book which would fill my mind with ideas completely separate from my pathetic concerns. And then I'd be more interesting, and Lars would like me better. And maybe I'd like myself better, and all would be good.

I downed the rest of my smoothie, took my glass to the sink, and headed upstairs. I had a lot to accomplish: it was time to get cracking.

By six-thirty, after a spa day of my own making, I was as good as I could be. Well, almost. I leaned toward my bathroom mirror and put the finishing touches on my makeup, which meant a dab of lip gloss, the tiniest bit of blush, and mainly a whole lot of staring at my reflection.

I looked okay, I decided. Glossy hair, pretty eyes, clear skin. I'd gone for a jog after my bath (which was stupid, as it meant a whole 'nother shower), but on the plus side, I felt healthy and strong. Even though, to be honest, it was more of a jog-walk-slog, complete with huffing and puffing and hatred of the many neighborhood hills. But I was exercising, that's what counted. I was a liberated, focused, exercise-loving girl. Yeah!

By seven, which was when Lars was supposed to be here, I was chilling on the sofa with Ty, watching *Hannah Montana* and working on the ironic smile I'd flash when Mom ushered Lars in. *I know, I know*, my expression would say when his eyebrows lifted at our choice of shows. *But what can I do? He's in second grade!*

I'd work in mention of my jog, too. Like, maybe when Miley was onstage strutting her stuff, I could say, "God, that's got to be such a good workout. And speaking of workouts . . ." Something like that?

By seven-thirty, I was ready for Lars to be here already. Why wasn't he? Had he gotten a flat tire? Ty and I were on our second episode of *Hannah Montana*, and it was nerve-racking staying so chill and relaxed. I did a quick dart to the bathroom to check my lip gloss, then scurried back to my hanging-out pose on the couch.

"Watch it," Ty said. "You almost made me spill my chocolate milk."

"Sorry," I said.

By eight-o-five, Lars still wasn't here, and Ty had switched the channel to TBS so he could watch *Full House*. He loved the littlest sister, Michelle, and fine, I did, too. She was cute, that single melded version of Mary-Kate and Ashley, who would later morph into gaunt, spooky club girls.

But an ironic smile could only stretch so far, and Lars catching me watching *Full House* was most likely beyond its limits. So I picked up the phone and called him, knowing it was the right thing to do, even though it made my palms sweaty.

"Um, hi, Mr. Mitchell," I said to his dad, who scared me. "Is Lars there?"

Mr. Mitchell didn't say "hello" back, but just put the phone down and bellowed, "Lars!" Which told me that Lars *was* there—*der*—and which made me abandon my flat-bike-tire theory. I gripped the phone.

"Winnie, hey!" Lars said when he picked up. He sounded absolutely normal: not sick, not wounded, not the slightest bit apologetic about not being here. Not even aware, as far as I could tell, that he was *supposed* to be here.

"Um . . ." I cleared my throat. "Weren't we . . . weren't you . . ."

"Oh, *crap*," he said. I could practically see him hitting his forehead, like someone on a sitcom would do. Like Miley's dad on *Hannah Montana* had in fact done only minutes ago, when Miley confronted him about an unsigned permission slip. Miley hadn't gotten to go on her field trip, all because of him.

"Winnie, I suck," Lars said. "I got busy on the computer and I completely spaced. I *suck*!"

"You don't suck," I said automatically. But in my brain, I thought, *You got busy on the computer?!*

"We'll catch our flick another time. Next weekend, okay?"

"It's only eight," I said.

"You're sweet. But nah, I'm not going to do that to you."

Do what to me? "I don't care. Just come over."

"How about Saturday? Saturday for sure."

I felt lost. I didn't want to make a big deal out of it—I didn't want to act desperate—but I didn't understand. Didn't he want to see me? Would he seriously rather kill time on the computer then sling his arm around me on the basement sofa and crack jokes about the ridiculous things the characters in the movie did?

"Okay," I heard myself say, because what else *could* I say? But he had let me down, again. And I wondered, as he told me I was the best and then got off the phone, when I was going to do anything about it.

The next morning, Cinnamon called in tears.

"Bryce broke up with me!" she wailed.

"Oh, Cinnamon!" I said. "No!"

"One week before Christmas," she said. "*One week before Christmas*. And I just bought him that sweater, that one from Abercrombie! And he was going to love it, he was going to look so good in it . . ." Sobs caught in her throat.

"Did he say why?" I asked. "Did you guys have a fight?"

"He did it on Facebook," she said. "That's how I found out. All of a sudden his status is listed as 'single,' and when I called him, he was like, 'Yeah, I wanted to tell you in person. Sorry.' "

I felt it like a blow in my gut, and I knew Cinnamon must be feeling it ten thousand times worse. "That is so lame," I said. "That is so *low*."

"Will you come over? I need you to come over."

"I'll be there in fifteen minutes."

I brought her a raspberry mocha from Starbucks—tricky to keep from spilling while on my bike, but that's the kind of stud I am—and I listened as she went over it again and again: how stunned she was, how shattered, how broken-hearted. How she hadn't seen it coming. How she would never fall in love again, never ever ever.

Dinah came over, too. She rubbed Cinnamon's back and said, "Maybe he'll realize he made a mistake."

Cinnamon gazed at Dinah with overly shiny eyes. Her lashes were damp with tears. "Do you think?" She turned to me. "People don't always mean it when they break up, do they? People get back together all the time!"

"Um . . ." I said. I wasn't sure how smart it was, encouraging this line of thought.

"Maybe he'll realize he had a temporary burst of insanity," Dinah said.

"Or maybe he won't," I said.

Cinnamon made a sound of indignation.

"I don't think you should falsely get your hopes up, that's all," I said.

"Not falsely," Cinnamon argued.

"Not falsely," Dinah agreed.

I gave Dinah a hard look, and she lifted her shoulders, like, *What am I supposed to do? This is our friend. She's hurting.*

"I just think . . ." I started.

"Yes, Miss I'm-in-a-Perfect-Relationship?" Cinnamon said.

I bristled. This wasn't about me. She shouldn't make it about me. But for her sake, I squashed my irritation.

"I just think you've got to believe a person when he says something," I said. I told them the whole story of last night and how Lars got too busy on the computer to come over. I offered it as a gift, to prove that my relationship with Lars *wasn't* perfect.

"But he said he'd make it up to me, so what was I supposed to do?" I finished. "I could harp on him and make him feel bad, or I could believe him and be like, 'Okay'."

Dinah seemed puzzled. "What does that have to do with Cinnamon and Bryce?"

"Are you saying I *harped* on him?" Cinnamon demanded. "And that's why he broke up with me?"

"What? No! I never—"

She tilted her head. "And Lars didn't get sucked into the Internet, or whatever he told you. He was hanging with Bryce. Bryce told me."

"Oh," I said. My heart did a flippy thing. "So . . . they both got sucked into the Internet. They were probably playing computer games."

"Nose-Ring Girl was there, too," Cinnamon said. Her expression had a burning quality to it. "And her friend. Stephanie. They dropped by in Nose-Ring Girl's MINI Cooper, Bryce said."

I tried to process this. Nose-Ring Girl? MINI Cooper? I'd seen her in it one day as she pulled into the high school parking lot, and it was blue and white, cute as a button. How was I supposed to compete with that?

"Bryce told you about his night and broke up with you, all in the same conversation?" Dinah asked.

Cinnamon raised her eyebrows. "Apparently so."

Tears sprang to my eyes. Lars had lied to me. He lied to me because he'd rather hang out with Nose-Ring Girl than me. *You're sweet,* he'd said. *You're the best.*

"Oh, Winnie," Dinah said, reaching over to rub *my* back.

Cinnamon went from looking as if she'd won something to looking as if she'd lost it right back again.

"Who knows?" she said dismally. "Maybe they'll both change their minds."

On Monday, Dinah and I protected Cinnamon from the evil Bryce, and Cinnamon and Dinah protected me from the evil Lars. Except he *wasn't* evil. He was Lars. And when he finally caught me on the quad without my bodyguards, he said, "Hey, babe. I looked for you after lunch. Where were you?"

I shrugged.

"I saved you this," he said, pulling a cookie wrapped in a napkin out of his jacket pocket.

"Gee, thanks," I said. He considered a cafeteria cookie some great gift?

"Aren't you going to take it? It's peanut butter. Your favorite."

"Peanut butter's not my favorite. Chocolate chip is."

"Second favorite, then." He tried to get me to make eye contact. "Winnie? You okay?"

I shrugged again.

"Win-nie," he cajoled. He tickled my ribs, slipping his hand inside my jacket and finding my most tender spot.

I pushed him away, but despite myself, I smiled. If only he weren't so cute! It would be a whole lot easier to stay mad at him if he weren't so cute.

He saw his advantage and ran with it, ducking in to steal a kiss. "Are we getting hot chocolate today?" he asked. Sometimes we walked to 7-Eleven after school and got hot chocolate from the machine. In warmer weather, Slurpees.

"I don't know, are we?" I said. "Or do you have other plans, like maybe getting sucked into the Internet again?"

Did I imagine it, or did he look nervous?

He did. He glanced away and folded his fingers over the cookie, which by now was probably crumbled.

Do it, I told myself. *Confront him about Nose-Ring Girl.*

If you don't, you're a total wimp and should be lashed with a whip.

"If you want hot chocolate, then I'm taking you out for hot chocolate," he said. "My treat."

"Ooo, big spender," I said. Hot chocolate from 7-Eleven was ninety-nine cents a cup.

"Anything for my girl," he said. He smiled, crookedly at first, and then with more confidence. He lashed me with the ol' Lars charm.

When I got home, full of hot chocolate but lacking a spine, I tried to figure out, again, why it was so hard to stand up for myself when it came to Lars. Was it because I liked him so much? Didn't want to lose him? Didn't want to be the girl who was dumped, like Cinnamon?

I found Ty in the basement making trophies out of duct tape. He had a whole collection; he'd gone duct tape crazy after the taping-up-his-pants incident last year. He'd made himself a duct tape vest and a duct tape ball cap, both of which he occasionally wore to school. *More power to him*, I'd finally decided.

"So how are things with Lexie?" I asked. I wanted to hear some good news in the realm of girl-boy relationships. More than that, I just wanted some sweet, innocent Ty love. Maybe that would make me feel less tainted. "Do you still like her?"

"Yes, I am in love with her, and she is in love with me,"

Ty said, intent on his trophy. He ripped off a piece of hot pink tape and wrapped it around the base. "But I do not like her friend."

"You mean Claire?"

"No, I like Claire. Who I don't like is her new friend, Breezie."

"Breezie? That's a cute name." I tried it out in my head: *Breezie Perry*. "Why don't you like Breezie?"

"Because."

"Because why?"

"She has a stench."

I giggled. "A *stench*?"

"It follows her around. Wherever she goes, there it is."

"Ty, be nice. Anyway, like you're really one to talk." Just this morning, as we were getting ready for school, he'd called me over and asked me to smell the air near his bottom.

"No way," I'd said. "Did you stink?"

"I don't know if I stank!" he protested. "That's why I need you to smell!"

"I don't mind my own stench," he said now. "Just Breezie's."

Well. This conversation wasn't giving me the warm fuzzies I'd hoped for. And "Breezie," come to think of it, was a terrible name for a girl with a stench problem. I officially crossed "Breezie" off my name list, since everyone had stenches once in a while.

"So how's Joseph doing?" I said, changing the subject. "Is he one of the Bad Scary Dry Cleaners?"

"No," Ty said. "Will you tear off a piece of black for me?"

I tore off a strip and stuck it to his arm. He pulled it free and placed it where it belonged.

"Another, please?"

I tore. I became his duct tape helper person. "Why isn't Joseph a Bad Scary Dry Cleaner? I thought you liked him."

"I do like him. He's just absent all the time."

I got a bad feeling. "What do you mean? Is he in the hospital? He hasn't dropped out of school, has he?"

"I don't know." He held out his hand. "Duct tape, please."

"But . . . that's awful!" I said. Chatting with Ty wasn't cheering me up one bit. "Joseph shouldn't be absent all the time. It's nearly Christmas! And Bryce shouldn't have broken up with Cinnamon! Christmas is supposed to be a happy time, not a time filled with sadness!"

Ty regarded me quizzically. "Duct tape, please?"

"Here," I said, doing several quick rips. "The rest you'll have to do yourself. I've got to go."

"Why?"

I pushed myself up from the carpet. My hair swished against my back; that's how long it had grown. The goal of cutting it for Locks of Love had floated around in my mind ever since June, popping up every so often and then submerging. But *could-have-would-have-should have*'s got you only so far.

"There's something I need to do," I said.

• • •

"You're sure about this?" the stylist said, her scissors poised over my head. A chunk of my hair draped over the fingers of her other hand, the requisite ten inches dangling down. Once she cut it, I'd go from being a long-haired girl to a short-haired girl. No more ponytails. No more messy French twists.

"I'm sure," I said.

The stylist looked at Mom for permission, as if Mom were the ultimate authority. It was irritating, because it was *my* hair. Sheesh.

"It's up to Winnie," Mom said.

"*Yes*," I said. "I'm sure. I've been sure for six months."

"You've been growing your hair out for six months?" Mom said. "And this was why?" She looked surprised and proud.

Warmth spread through me. Lars might be shocked—he might not even like it—but did I care?

"Well, I think it's wonderful what you're doing, and it sure will make a difference in someone's life," the stylist said. She closed the blades of her scissors and claimed the first ten-inch chunk. "It's hard to feel good about yourself when you don't feel pretty. We all know it's the inside that counts—but the outside matters, too, doesn't it?"

"So true," Mom said, who'd been complaining more and more about feeling fat.

"Will it be turned into a wig in time for Christmas?" I

asked. My chest was tight with the scariness of seeing my hair go away, but I was breathing. I was okay.

"I don't know, hon," the stylist said. She kept clipping. "But one day soon some lucky little girl is going to receive it, and it's sure to be her best present ever."

January

TY *LOVED* HIS CHRISTMAS LIZARD. Loved it, loved it, loved it. He named it Sneaky Bob Lizard, and he took it everywhere with him: to the dinner table, to the bathtub (Sneaky Bob didn't get in, but he kept watch from the counter), to bed. It made me happy.

On the morning of our first day back to school after break, Ty and Sneaky Bob joined me in my bathroom so we could chat as I got ready. Ty sat on the closed toilet; Sneaky Bob sat on Ty. Sneaky Bob's yellow eyes watched my every move.

"She is giving herself her beauty treatment," Ty told Sneaky Bob as I stroked on a smidgen of the cool pink eye shadow Sandra had given me for Christmas. She'd given me a whole goodie bag of Sephora stuff, all different brands. I especially liked the "Bad Gal" mascara with its super-fat wand.

"Now she's making herself smell good," he said as I spritzed the air with vanilla perfume and walked through it.

"Something your owner should look into," I told Sneaky Bob.

"Okey-doke," Ty said, hopping off the toilet. I aimed the perfume bottle at him, but he said he could do it himself.

Ah, well, I thought. *A hint of vanilla never hurt a boy.* He spritzed a second time and whizzed Sneaky Bob through the mist. *Or a lizard.*

"Hey, Winnie," Ty said. "How many frogs would fit in lizard's stomach?"

"Hmm. A real lizard, or Sneaky Bob?"

"Sneaky Bob *is* real," Ty said.

"Well, yeah. I was talking size, though. Sneaky Bob's bigger than most lizards."

"How many frogs would fit in Sneaky Bob's stomach. That's what I need to know."

I imagined frogs the size of fists. I chunked them mentally into Sneaky Bob's belly. "Three," I said.

"And how many bugs can one frog eat?"

"Hmm. Fifteen?"

"So what is fifteen plus fifteen plus fifteen?"

"You figure it out." He was smart. He just didn't always know it.

"Forty-five," he said, pleased. "That means Sneaky Bob can eat forty-five bugs." He patted Sneaky Bob's head. "Good Sneaky Bob."

I put on the dangly blue and green earrings that were my present from Lars and swished my head to feel their weight. They were beautiful. At first I worried they'd look freakish with my short hair—I was accustomed to dangly earrings with long hair—but Cinnamon and Dinah had assured me that they actually looked better with my chin-length bob. More dramatic. More sophisticated.

"What do you think?" I said, turning to Ty for his approval.

"Pretty," he said. He tilted his face, offering up his cheek. "Kiss?"

I gave him a smooch—was there ever a sweeter brother than Ty?—and bestowed an additional smooch on Sneaky Bob.

"Gotta go, dudes," I told the two of them. "Don't eat too many flies."

Cinnamon and Dinah had a theory: Lars was the perfect boyfriend when we were alone; it was only when Nose-Ring Girl was around that he forgot how to treat me right. I hated to admit it, but it was maybe kind of true.

My goal on this first day back was to help Lars set a new pattern. New year, new pattern—it was fully within the realm of possibility.

How exactly I was going to do this, I hadn't figured out. Basically the plan was to get to him first, before Nose-Ring Girl appeared on the scene, and just exist as my cool, laid-back self. I'd have on the earrings he gave me, which would remind him of our fabulous "just us" time over break, and I wouldn't let myself get cowed if Nose-Ring Girl did show up. I'd take Lars's hand. I'd be confident. If I felt like snuggling against him, well, then I would. Why not?

Flanked by Cinnamon and Dinah, I went to see Lars before first period. This was ballsy of us, as it meant hunting him down in the Boys' School, which was the old-school name for the building on campus where the high school guys had homeroom. At eight-ten, they'd join the girls for their actual classes, but during homeroom, it was testosterone city.

Cinnamon was nervous as we opened the heavy door and stepped into the first floor hall.

"What if we see Bryce?" she said.

"Then we'll glare at him like the snake he is," I said. Cinnamon had gone ahead and given Bryce the Abercrombie sweater—bad move—but it hadn't softened his heart. Louise later told us that she'd seen Bryce wearing it at the mall, the day before New Year's Eve. He'd been with Stephanie, Nose-Ring Girl's crony. *Hiss.*

"I don't want to see him," Cinnamon said. "I'm not ready."

"His locker's at the other end of the hall from Lars's," I reminded her. I clutched her arm. "Look—there he is!"

"Who? Bryce?" she said, hyperventilating.

"Lars," I said. "Doesn't he look adorable?" He was wearing his new "Life Is Good" shirt, which I'd decided in the end was a better present for him than for Dinah and Cinnamon. I'd felt a teensy bit guilty, like I was selling out by putting him ahead of them, but that wasn't it at all. He was hard to buy for, and a "Life Is Good" shirt was quirky and just the right amount of intimate without going overboard.

Dinah and Cinnamon were easy to buy for. Plus, it wasn't like they knew I'd switched their gift idea over to Lars. All they knew was that I'd given them lovely almond-scented shampoo and conditioner from The Body Shop. They were most appreciative.

"Aww!" Dinah said. "That color looks awesome on him."

It did, it did. The shirt I'd selected was forest green, soft and faded, with a smiley stick figure guy on skis, since Lars loved to ski.

My heart rate quickened. "Lars!" I said when we were within feet of him. "Hey!"

He turned from his locker, and his face lit up. "Winnie! Nice earrings."

"Nice shirt," I retorted. He pulled me close, circling his arm around my waist.

He said "hey" to Cinnamon and Dinah, and he wasn't weird toward Cinnamon, which was good. He didn't mention Bryce. Neither did she. The four of us groaned about school being back in session and the prospect of getting our finals back, and the whole time, his arm stayed around me.

And then it left. His arm. He pulled away from me, and my throat closed. Nose-Ring Girl was heading our way.

"Doesn't she know this is the Boys' School?" Dinah whispered in my ear. "What is she doing here?"

Apparently, the same thing we were: visiting Lars. She

gave him a teasing smile, a stupid, tenth-grade, *I'm so cool* smile, and I tried to keep my expression impassive. But nervousness made my armpits suddenly damp.

"Hey, mister," she said to Lars. She said not one word to me or Cinnamon or Dinah. She didn't even comment on my hair, although she had to have noticed. (Lars, for the record, had tousled my newly short hair two days after I got it cut and said I looked terrific. "But you'd look terrific no matter what," he'd said.)

"Hi, Brianna," I said, just to prove I could. Yes, her name was Brianna. Now *that* was a bad name. A conceited, self-centered, boyfriend-stealing name. I'd continue to call her Nose-Ring Girl, thanks very much.

"Hi," she said with no eye contact. She bumped Lars's hip. "Great party Friday, huh?"

Party? What party? "I thought you went out with the guys on Friday," I said.

"Um, I did," he said, looking uncomfortable.

"Yeah, to Stephanie's party," Nose-Ring Girl said. "Her parents were out of town. We did Jell-O shooters."

"What's a Jell-O shooter?" Dinah asked.

Nose-Ring Girl glanced at her. She laughed.

The warning bell rang, and Lars raked his hand through his hair. "You better go," he said to me. "You've got to make it all the way over to the junior high building."

Nose-Ring Girl laughed again, with a snortish sound mixed in.

I felt helpless. I wanted to give Lars a quick kiss, to claim him as mine, but there was just too much in the air.

"Call me?" I said.

"You bet," he said.

"Promise?"

Nose-Ring Girl rolled her eyes.

"I said I would," Lars said.

I felt like an idiot.

"Come on, Winnie," Dinah said. "Let's go."

I had to fight not to look back over my shoulder.

The next day I skipped lunch, heading instead to the collection of Dumpsters behind the cafeteria. No one was supposed to go back there. It was smelly and shadowy and littered with cigarette butts, which you never never *never* saw on the rest of Westminster's campus. Where the Dumpsters lived was the dark underbelly of the school—and leaning against the back wall of the cafeteria, one foot propped on the bricks, was Amanda.

I'd heard she'd started hanging out back here. I hadn't believed it. Or maybe I had, because I'd wandered back here to find her, hadn't I?

"Um . . . hi," I said.

If Amanda was surprised, she didn't show it. She was still doing the heavy-eyeliner thing, and she'd dyed her lovely Alice in Wonderland hair a flat, matte black. Her mode of being was to remain unimpressed at all times, a posture she pulled off admirably.

"Hey," she said, neither friendly nor unfriendly. She had an inked in drawing of a rose on her wrist, I noticed. The petals, like her hair, were black.

Are you happy? I suddenly wanted to ask. But I didn't. Even *I* wasn't that idiotic.

Her buddy, Aubrey, regarded me with the same impassive expression as Amanda. Aubrey had joined the Amanda-Gail-Malena crowd around the end of last semester, but now it seemed as if Amanda and Aubrey had split off and formed their own Goth duo.

"Um, can I ask you a question?" I said.

"I guess," Amanda said.

I wanted to ask her alone, without Aubrey watching me like a lizard. (Only not a nice lizard, like Sneaky Bob.) But apparently that wasn't going to happen.

"Did you go to Stephanie's party on Saturday?"

She nodded, slowly. "I was there."

"She told her mom she was spending the night with me," Aubrey said. She sniggered. "Which was true. We just didn't watch *The Sound of Music* like we said we did."

A twisty smile cracked Amanda's expression, and I thought without meaning to of Mrs. Wilson and her cashmere sweater sets.

Would I lie to Mom one day? Would there ever be a situation when I'd need to? Even if I did need to, I didn't know that I'd be able to pull it off. My gut hurt just thinking about it.

Then again, I sometimes lied to Mom about wearing my

bike helmet. And my homework. And whose granola bar wrapper was crumpled plain as day on the floor by the sofa.

Well. Not *important* stuff, though.

"Um . . . was Lars there?" I asked. "At Stephanie's party?"

Amanda nodded again. "Brianna was hanging all over him, as usual. She's so trashy."

My heart sank. I was also engulfed with shame, as if it were my fault, which was so wrong and false that I hated myself for it.

"Did he . . . seem to like it?" I asked. "I mean, not *like* it, but, you know, encourage it. Encourage *her*." My cheeks burned. "Not tell her 'no'."

Aubrey was amused, which killed me. I hated Aubrey. Bad Aubrey. *Stupid, lizard-eyed, above-it-all Aubrey, who had split ends and didn't even know it.*

Amanda shot Aubrey a look, and for that split second I had the sense that the Amanda I once knew still existed, even if she was buried beneath hair dye and black eyeliner. Amanda's look said *stop it*, and Aubrey did.

"He didn't tell her 'no'," Amanda told me. "But he didn't reciprocate."

"Oh," I said.

"Guys are like that. They don't know *how* to say no." She hitched up one shoulder. "That doesn't mean he isn't into you."

"I know," I said. But I also knew that being "into me" wasn't enough. Which sucked, because now I could no longer pretend it was.

• • •

"Winnie," Ty said, poking my shoulder repeatedly. "Winnie!"

"*What*, Ty?" I was slumped next to him on the couch, my eyes tracking Timmy Turner as he battled a squadron of what appeared to be roaches. Ty sat criss-cross-applesauce on top of a pile of throw pillows, Sneaky Bob in his lap. I knew he thought I was being a poop, but I was there beside him, wasn't I? I'd told him I'd watch TV with him, and I, for one, was true to my word. Did he expect me to hold a conversation with him, too?

"Want some Skittles?" he said.

"What I *want* is for Lars to call me," I said. "He promised he would, but he hasn't. Why hasn't he called?"

"I have no idea." He dangled his candy in front of me. "Skittles?"

I focused on the neon green package. Sour Skittles—not my fave. I wasn't hungry anyway.

"No, thanks."

"Say 'yes'," he said.

"Fine. Yes."

He jerked the Skittles away, holding them as far away from me as his arm would allow. "Ha ha, tricked you!"

I regarded him with infinite hurt and betrayal, far more than the situation called for. I was fully aware I was doing it, and I felt fully justified, too. He had acted unkindly. Unkind behavior called for reprisal.

Ty's brown eyes went wide. "No, wait, you can have some. Hold out your hand."

"It's too late," I said.

Ty's lower lip quivered, which not everyone would have noticed. But I did, because I was the best at knowing when he was upset. Like if he saw a dead squirrel or something, I knew he'd worry about it and want me to say a prayer with him. "I hope you are happy in heaven," he'd say, peeking at my face to make sure I was praying, too. "Amen."

"Just push that joke away," he said. He reached over and pressed on my lower lip, which was jutted out in an exaggerated pout. "And push that face away!"

I ignored him. His breath got fast. Yes, it hurt me, too, but tough.

"Winnie?" Mom said, clopping into the den in the clogs she'd taken to wearing. The pregnancy was making her feet swell, and clogs worked better than her normal high heels. "Can I talk to you for a sec?"

Great, I thought, expecting to get scolded for being mean to Ty.

But when I followed her into the hall, Mom took my hand and said, "Baby, I need you to do something for me. I need you to go with Ty to the hospital."

My stomach dropped out of my body. "What? Why?"

"To visit Joseph."

I must have looked blank—which I was, but not for the reason she thought—because she said, "His friend who's so sick?"

"No, I know who he is." I tried to get my act together. "Why's he in the hospital?"

Mom squeezed my hand. "He's not doing well, Winnie. None of the treatments have done what they hoped."

Oh, no, I thought. "But he's not . . . I mean, he's not going to—"

"I hope not. But Joseph's mom let Mrs. Webber know that Joseph would appreciate visitors, and I think that's a really nice idea. I'd take Ty myself"—she glanced at her watch—"but Mimi from my prenatal group is throwing me a surprise baby shower. I have to be there."

"A *surprise* baby shower?"

"Well, it's supposed to be a surprise," she said. "But this is my fourth time on the baby train, you know. I know the signs."

"Couldn't you take Ty tomorrow?"

"Tomorrow's not good. Joseph has chemo."

"I thought you said the treatments weren't working."

She sighed.

"Mom?"

"It's complicated. And honestly, if it were one of you . . ."

"If it was one of us, what?"

"Chemo is hard. Hard on the kids, hard on the parents." She paused. "But sometimes, I guess, it's even harder to give up."

I didn't want to think about that. I refused to think about that. "There could always be a miracle," I said.

"That's true," she said. "There could always be a miracle."

The hallway where we stood was dark, even though it was only four o'clock. This part of the house always got dark first, because there were no windows. I could see Mom's face, but it was difficult to read her expression.

"Winnie . . . do you not *want* to go with Ty to visit Joseph?"

I stubbed my sock-footed toe on the hardwood floor. What was I supposed to say? *It's not that, it's just that I don't want to miss a call from my boyfriend, who doesn't know how to tell other girls he's taken?*

"It doesn't have to be a long visit," Mom went on. "I'd drop you guys off on my way to Mimi's, and then Dad would pick you up on his way home from work. You'd be there probably an hour."

I was such a jerk. Such a pathetic loser for caring about my own problems when Joseph's were so much worse.

"Joseph's mom doesn't want him to get tired out, anyway," Mom said.

"Okay, yes, I'll go," I said.

"Great," Mom said. She stepped into the den and projected her voice. "Ty, want to go visit Joseph at the hospital?"

Ty turned from the TV. First he looked at me to see if I was still mad at him, and when he saw I wasn't, he untangled his legs. "Can I bring Sneaky Bob?"

"Sure," Mom said. Her expression went soft as she watched him slide down from his pile of pillows, and her hand—the one not holding mine—went to her rounded belly. I don't know if she even realized it.

"Grab your jackets, you two," she said. "It's cold out."

•••

Joseph's hospital room was pale blue with a border of clown wallpaper. A bouquet of miniature balloons on plastic sticks sat on the table, along with a slew of teddy bears and get-well cards. *Get well*, as if it were Joseph's choice and he just had to snap to it. I know nobody meant anything cruel by the cards, or anything other than *We love you, we're thinking about you, we're praying for you.* But seeing them all jaunty on the table made me feel like the world was a sad, sad place. I wasn't very good at sadness.

"Dad'll be here soon to pick you up," Mom said, kissing the top of Ty's head. She smiled tentatively at Mrs. Strand, Joseph's mother.

"I've got to run," Mom told her, "but Winnie's going to stay and hang out with the boys. She's very responsible, if you want to get a cup of coffee or something."

Mrs. Strand nodded. Circles shadowed her eyes. "I could use some coffee. I think I will." She looked at Joseph. "Joseph? If you need juice, or more crackers, just ask Winnie, all right?"

"Or me," Ty said. So far he'd stayed glued to my side, but now he edged closer to the metal railings of Joseph's bed.

"And push the call button if you feel like you need Nurse Anna to come check on you," Mrs. Strand said.

"Mo-o-om," Joseph said. He was upright in his bed, propped on two pillows. His red knit cap looked bigger than it used to. His eyebrows no longer existed, I guess because of the chemo, and his skin was raw and rashy.

"All right, all right," Mrs. Strand said in the martyred tone of mothers everywhere. "It's just that I love you, that's all."

"I *know*," Joseph said.

Finally the grown-ups left, and it was just me, Ty, and Joseph.

"So, um, how are you feeling?" I asked, and immediately hated myself. How was that any better than *Get well soon*?

"Okay," Joseph said. His arm was rashy, just like his face. He scratched it.

"I like your shirt," Ty said. It was dark blue with a bright yellow sun on it, and underneath was the word HOTLANTA.

"Thanks," Joseph said in a monotone.

Well this is going to be fun for all of us, I thought to myself.

Ty walked over to Joseph's bed and held up Sneaky Bob. "This is Sneaky Bob Lizard. He's a lizard." Then, realizing how he'd repeated himself, Ty thwacked his head. "Duh!"

"Is he a Komodo Dragon lizard?" Joseph asked.

"Probably. You can hold him, but he's heavy." Ty heaved Sneaky Bob over the rail and dropped him on Joseph's chest.

"*Ooof*," Joseph said, just as I cried, "Ty!" I rushed over, but Joseph was grinning under the weight of Sneaky Bob.

Joseph hefted Sneaky Bob onto the bed rail and said, "Watch this." He nudged Sneaky Bob's abdomen, and Sneaky Bob fell to the floor with a satisfying thud.

Ty cackled. He snatched Sneaky Bob up and balanced him

on the rail at the bottom of the bed, which was higher than the side rails. "Geronimo!" he exclaimed, shoving Sneaky Bob off.

"Don't be too rough," I warned. "He'll pop, and beans will fly everywhere."

"Beans?" Joseph said.

"No, poop!" Ty said, thrusting Sneaky Bob in Joseph's face. "Poop will fly everywhere and hit you in the eye!"

"*Ty*!" I said.

"And pee," Joseph said. He reached down and wiggled a clear plastic bag hanging from an IV pole. It was half full of a pale yellow liquid; I suddenly realized what it was. "My pee bag will explode and pee will go everywhere!"

I made the sign of the cross, partly for effect and partly for real. Ty and Joseph were deep in seven-year-old-boy land; nothing I could do was going to save me. "Gross, you guys!"

The poop became a poop mountain; the pee became a pee ocean. And then somehow a Poop and Pee Airline was invented to fly travelers to Poop Mountain and Pee Ocean, although the code name for the airline was Dolphin Airlines, to keep the unsuspecting from being tipped off.

Um . . . *yeah*. I backed away slowly and carefully and vowed to beware any airlines named for sea mammals.

Mrs. Strand returned just as Sneaky Bob took a death-defying plunge off the table, his tail lashing the cards into a pile of invisible poop. Ty and Joseph guffawed. Mrs. Strand's eyebrows shot up.

I hopped out of the chair.

"Oh, gosh, I'm so sorry," I said. I knelt to gather the cards.

"Don't worry," Mrs. Strand said.

"I don't think they hurt anything—I mean, well, except for the cards, but—"

"Winnie," Mrs. Strand said. "Seriously, it's fine."

I raised my head and saw that she meant it. In one hand she held a box of granola bars, and in the other a plastic-wrapped ten-pack of juice boxes. She looked different than when we'd first gotten here. Not happier, exactly, but once again ready to take it on, the pain and unfairness her child was going through.

Joseph's chortling helped. I saw it in her eyes.

When we left twenty minutes later, Sneaky Bob stayed behind. Ty checked with me first, clutching my shirt and yanking me to his level.

"Ow," I complained.

"I think Sneaky Bob wants to stay here," he whispered.

"You do?"

"With Joseph. But I don't want to hurt your feelings."

For just a second, it did hurt my feelings. Which was crazy. And then that selfishness went away, and I thought, *Oh, Ty*.

"You want to give Sneaky Bob to Joseph? Forever?" I asked.

He nodded. His fingers tightened around Sneaky Bob's

green scales, and I knew he honestly did want to. I also knew he was already missing him.

"It won't hurt my feelings," I said.

So Ty gave Sneaky Bob to Joseph, who propped him beside him on the overstuffed hospital pillow. At first Mrs. Strand got all motherish and said, "No, no." But she relented when the faces of both boys fell.

"Well . . . all right," she said. "Thank you, Ty. That was very, very nice." She turned to Joseph. "Joseph, is there anything you want to say?"

"Poop," Joseph said solemnly.

He and Ty fell to pieces.

It was after six by the time we got home. Ty turned on the kitchen lights while Dad plonked the McDonald's bags on the table and lifted out burgers and fries. Sandra was having dinner with Bo, and Mom was still at her baby shower, so Dad, Ty, and I were feasting on quarter pounders and fries.

Only, I didn't know if I was hungry. Maybe yes, maybe no. The red light on the answering machine was blinking: it all depended on what happened when I pressed the "PLAY" button.

I pressed. Mom's voice filled the kitchen, reminding Dad of the new McDonald's rule, which was that we had to get milk, chocolate milk, or O.J. as our drink, as if that would balance out the vats of grease in our meals.

"Too late!" crowed Ty, slurping his Coke.

Next came a message from Sandra's friend, Elise. Boring.

And that was it. Just those two messages, no more. I checked caller ID, to see if Lars had called but not left a message. He hadn't.

Well. That was that, then. The kitchen felt empty without the hustle-and-bustle cheerfulness of Mom. Sandra, if she were here, would either be grouchy and sullen or hilariously cheeky, and I missed her, too. The smell of cheese and dead cow wrapped around me.

"Winnie, come sit down," Dad said. "Your quarter pounder's getting cold."

"I will," I said, knowing I wouldn't. "I've just got to make a call first, okay?"

I went to the den so I could talk in private. *If* he was even there. If he wasn't over at Stephanie's or Brianna's for another wild blowout.

"Mitchell residence," Lars said when he answered, because he thought it was a corny-cool way to pick up.

I said nothing. I felt dead inside, which was so dumb. I wasn't dead. I wasn't even sick. There were so many things in the world that were more important than my pathetic problems, and yet here they were anyway: my pathetic problems, making me feel dead inside.

"Yo," Lars said. "Hola! Anyone there?"

"It's me," I said.

"Winnie!" he said, sounding, as always, happy to hear from me.

"You didn't call. You promised you'd call, and you didn't."

He laughed. Not a real laugh, but a defensive "guy" laugh.

"I was going to," he said. "It's, like, seven-thirty! The night is young!"

I waited.

"I was watching CNN with my dad. World issues, man. Big, big, big."

I blinked back tears. I didn't want to be this nagging freak-girl. I didn't like the way it made me feel, the way it changed me.

"You have to be nicer to me," I said.

Again, he laughed. "What? I'm King of Nice. What are you talking about?"

"You have to be nicer to me, or . . . or . . ."

"Or what?" he said. Still Lars, still charming and jokey, but with a thread of fear. It snaked in and pierced my numbness and almost broke my resolve. Almost, but not quite.

"Or I have to break up with you," I whispered.

What more was there to say? Nothing. So I hung up.

February

VALENTINE'S DAY *SUCKED*. Seriously, it was the meanest, suckiest holiday ever. If you had a boyfriend, then Valentine's Day was fine and dandy and chocolate candy. But if you didn't? Then lucky you, you got to skulk about in your cloud of loser-ness as blissful couples gamboled like fawns and flung rosebuds into the air.

It was a gloater's holiday, that's what it was. It encouraged people to gloat, gloat, gloat. *Look at me! I'm happy! Look at me! I'm loved!*

But I wasn't happy, and I wasn't loved, and as I trudged through the motions of getting ready for school, I wished I could push a fast-forward button and skip over Valentine's Day entirely. Ever since Lars and I broke up—which I guess is what we did, although that wasn't what I wanted—school had been nothing but misery. Whenever I saw Lars in the halls or on the quad, Cinnamon yanked my arm and pulled me the opposite direction. She said Lars was a jerk, just like Bryce, and that I was better off without him.

"He has to prove himself to you," she said. "And he hasn't, so he doesn't get to talk to you."

"But what if I want to talk to him?" I asked.

"Too bad," she said.

Dinah was kinder. Dinah said that Lars liked me, she knew he did, but that he hadn't learned to be the sort of person he had it within himself to be. Or something like that. She agreed that he had to come to me, though.

"He kind of has to," she said, scrinching her face like she knew it wasn't what I wanted to hear.

So, yeah. School sucked. Today would be even more miserable than usual, because of Valentine's Day carnations. Last year, Lars sent me a pink carnation. We were young and innocent and hadn't even kissed yet—hadn't even held hands!—but he sent me a pink carnation, and I floated on air.

This year, there would be no pink carnations, and their absence would be a blinking neon light above my head. A blinking light of sadness as deep as my bones.

Ty wandered into my room as I gloomily tugged on a pair of black hose to go with my black skirt and shirt. I figured I was in mourning, so I might as well dress like it.

"Those are ugly," he commented, regarding my floppy stocking feet. He plopped onto my bed. "They look like rotten elephant trunks."

"Gee, thanks," I said.

"I wouldn't wear those ugly things if I were you. I would take them off and throw them in the trash."

"Well, when I want fashion advice from a seven-year-old, I'll ask for it," I snapped.

His expression faltered. "Why are you being mean?"

"*I'm* not being mean—you are. You're the one coming in here and telling me how ugly I am!"

"Not you! Your stockings!" He looked worried, the way he always got when he thought someone was mad at him.

"It's the same thing. Saying my stockings are ugly is the same as saying I'm ugly, so you should think about that next time before you start insulting someone." It was working—I was making him feel as bad as I did—only it didn't feel as good as I'd hoped. So I tried to soften it. "Okay, Tyler-poo?"

His breaths quickened. "You called me poop! You called me poop!"

"What? No, I didn't."

"Poo is poop, so you did, too!"

Oh God. Why had I bothered?

"Ty, give it up," I said. "You're acting like a baby."

"Nuh-uh, Winifred-vomit."

"Uh-huh, Tyler-dirty-belly-button."

"Nuh-*uh*, Winnie-diarrhea!" Ty cried. He got to his feet, hands balled into fists. "Nuh-uh, Winnie-dirty-bagina!"

I gaped. I knew I wasn't being the best big sister . . . but calling someone a dirty bagina?

"Ty, you need to apologize," I said sharply.

"*You* need to apologize!"

"No, you do. And if you're not going to, you need to shut up and get out of my room."

Ty looked shocked. Then came the tears. Big floppy tears that didn't spill out, but just welled in his eyes, giving him the appearance of an abused orphan.

I felt bad, but it was a twisty, pissy kind of bad. The world was a hard, cold place—how would he ever survive if one measly "shut up" could bring him to tears?!

"It is weird," he whispered. "I miss you, but you're right here."

"Yeah, well, I won't be forever," I said. "No one will. And then how will you feel, huh?" There was a stabbing in my heart as I pointed to the door. "Now leave."

In the front seat of Sandra's car, as we drove to Westminster, I stared out the window with my head resting against the glass. A line from a Dr. Seuss book played through my head: *Gray Day. Everything is gray. I watch. But nothing moves today*.

Sandra flicked on the turn signal as we approached the school, and I sighed.

"Could we just not?" I said. "Couldn't we skip, just this once?"

Sandra glanced at me. The two of us hadn't spoken for the whole ride, and I got the sense she wasn't in the greatest mood, either—probably because Bo was out of town visiting the University of South Carolina.

She bit the corner of her lip . . . then did the strangest thing. She flicked the turn signal off. I lifted my head. I sat up straight and watched, amazed, as we passed Westminster's front gate.

"Are you serious?" I said. Excitement filled me, but anxiety, too. "We'll get busted! We'll totally get suspended!"

"For skipping one day? I don't think so," Sandra said. "But just in case, hand me my cell."

I fished for it in her bag and gave it to her. She dialed four-one-one and requested Westminster's main number. Once connected, she asked to be put through to the girls' school.

"Hey there," she said smoothly, taking on the "phone voice" Mom used and which Sandra always mocked. "This is Ellen Perry, and I just wanted to let you know that Sandra and Winnie won't be coming in today. I'm afraid they've both got a stomach bug."

Holy pickles, holy pickles! I held frozen in my seat. There was spazziness inside me, but I held it in tight.

"Oh, I *know*," Sandra was saying. She really did sound freakily like Mom. "Mmm-hmm. I hope so, too. Yes, I certainly will—thanks so much!"

She clapped shut her phone and looked at me victoriously. I screamed.

"Omigod, Sandra!" I said, bouncing like crazy. "You are so awesome! You are the best big sister ever! Omi*god*!!!"

She tried to play it cool, but her lips curved up despite herself. "I am, aren't I?" She opened her phone back up and hit the "off" button. Its farewell tinkle let us know it was shutting down. "There, now we can't be bothered even if someone tries."

I leaned back in my seat. I soaked in the glorious blue of the sky. Then I turned, beaming, to Sandra and said, "So . . . what should we do? We can't go home, obviously."

"And we can't go to school," she said.

I giggled. No Valentine's Day hoopla! No terrible, ugly carnations! No worrying about passing Lars in the hall and seeing him with evil Brianna! I was fizzy with adrenaline.

"Let's go to the butterfly center," I said. I'd always wanted to go to the butterfly center, where butterflies supposedly flitted everywhere and landed on your shoulders and hair and outstretched hands.

"The butterfly center is all the way out by Callaway Gardens," Sandra said. "That's, like, over an hour away."

"So? We have all day!"

She shook her head. "We're not going to the butterfly center."

"Then how about the Georgia Aquarium? We can pet the sharks!" They were teeny sharks, teeny sand sharks which could never eat a human in their life, but so? It was still cool to stroke their sinuous bodies.

"I don't think so," Sandra said, as if it was a stupid idea and she was just barely refraining from saying so. It made me feel childish instead of grown-up, which was so not the point on a day of skipping school.

"Okay . . . what do *you* want to do?" I asked, trying to

sound less hyper. I sure didn't want her deciding she'd made a mistake.

"I'm hungry. Let's go to Katz's Deli."

Eww, I thought. *Katz's Deli?* Katz's Deli was where old ladies went. Katz's Deli sold lox. But I nodded and said, "Sure. Yum."

At our table, over bagels with roast beef and Muenster cheese, Sandra unloaded about spring semester and how stressful it was and how she was already so sad about going to college and leaving all her friends behind.

"Well, not *behind*," she amended. "It's not like they're staying in Atlanta while I march bravely forth. But that's what's so depressing! Everyone's just going their own directions!" She counted off on her fingers. "Elizabeth's going to UNC; she got the Rhodes Scholarship. Raelynn's almost definitely going to Carlton, and Tess is going to Stanford. Which is in California, which is all the way across the country! At best I'll see her over Christmas break. How wrong is that?"

"Um . . . pretty wrong?" I said. Tess was nice—she gave me a pair of hand-me-down jeans that were too small for her or any of the other seniors—but Sandra had only just started being friends with her this year. I couldn't see how Tess moving to California was *that* big a tragedy.

"And Bo . . ." she said. She sighed and put down her bagel sandwich, which she'd taken one small bite of.

Ahhh. Bo. Yes, that was the real tragedy. Bo was Sandra's

love, and now they were going to be torn apart like Romeo and Juliet.

I used to have a love.

I still *did* have a love. He just didn't have me.

"Is Bo going to USC for sure?" I asked.

"Pretty sure," Sandra said. She tugged free a piece of roast beef and played with it, turning it over and over. "They're offering him baseball money. It would be hard to turn down."

"And you for sure want to go to Middlebury," I stated. Middlebury, which was in Vermont, was Sandra's top choice, and Sandra's college counselor said things looked good for Sandra getting accepted. As in, she'd be shocked if Sandra didn't.

"Yeah," Sandra said morosely.

The thought which ran through my head was, *But if you're so depressed about it . . . why go? Why not go to USC, too? And then just visit Vermont to go skiing or whatever.*

But I stayed silent and tried to look understanding. It was rare that Sandra talked to me like this, straight and real as if we were on the same level.

"Sometimes I wonder if he and I should just go ahead and break up now," Sandra said. "Do you know how few high school relationships last? Like, none. Seriously, maybe one out of a zillion."

"But you guys could be that one," I said. I sipped my lemonade, careful not to slurp. I took a delicate bite of my sandwich, which was difficult, given its bagel-ness. Bagel sandwiches were very mouth-stretching, and once the bite was claimed, you had to chew and chew and chew.

"Sometimes I don't even know if I *want* us to last," she said.

Now I was glad my mouth was full of bagel, so I didn't have to respond. She and Bo, not together . . . ? I couldn't even imagine.

"I'm supposed to stay with my very first boyfriend forever?" she went on. "And not date anyone else? And get married, and have kids, and never know what it's like to go out with someone else?"

"But—" I tried to shift some of the bagel glop around to make room for words. "If you *love* him—"

"I do love him! He's the love of my life!" She looked tormented. "Only . . . what if he *isn't*?"

I was amazed that Sandra was saying this. Amazed, too, that her fear was what if *he* isn't, not *what if I'm not*. Not *What if Bo finds someone else? What if he stops loving me? What if he's the love of my life, but I'm not the love of his?*

A question rose up, and I tried to figure out how to ask it, because I wanted to learn from Sandra while I still could. Because she wouldn't just be leaving Bo and her friends when she went to Vermont. She'd be leaving me, too. Which was so incomprehensible—a house without Sandra?—that I didn't really know how to process it.

"How did you . . . you know . . ."

She wrinkled her brow. "How did I what?"

I swallowed. *Finally.* "How did you . . . make him love you?"

The minute it was out, the very *second* it was out, I regretted it. *How did you make him love you?!*

"Never mind," I said quickly. My face burned, and I took another bite of sandwich to fill my stupid mouth.

But Sandra was kind. She knew what I was really asking, which wasn't about Bo. It was about Lars. What did I do wrong?

She gazed at me. "Oh, Winnie. It sucks, doesn't it?"

My throat tightened, because it *did* suck. I loved Sandra for saying it. For not making me feel like a baby.

Sandra peered at the piece of roast beef she'd been fooling with. She frowned.

"What?" I said.

"Is roast beef supposed to glisten?" She twisted it to make it catch the light, and I saw what she was talking about. There was a rainbow sheen on the meat, little scales of fluorescence. She drew the beef to her nose and sniffed. "Eww."

I spit out the chunk in my mouth. The big chunk. The other chunks, the ones already swallowed, roiled in my stomach and cast up the cry of rotting meat.

"Gross," Sandra said, observing the half-chewed mass on my plate.

There was an extreme likeliness of throwing-up in my

near future, which Sandra must have read on my face. She pointed to the bathroom at the back of the restaurant and said, "Go."

I scooched back my chair and ran.

As far as exciting, glamorous, *look-at-us-we're-ditching* adventures go, our day was pretty much a bust. Sandra was depressed, and so was I. Plus I smelled like vomit. Not hugely so, not so much that an innocent bystander would have breathed in and gagged, but enough to linger in my awareness. I'd made it to the deli's bathroom, but just barely, and a little of the barf had splattered on my shirt. I'd scrubbed it with water and soap, but still. The stink of throw-up was hard to shake.

We'd gone from the deli to the mall, where we moped around and felt bludgeoned by commercialism. There were lots of moms and strollers, more so than in my normal mall-going hours, and while the babies were cute, seeing them parade by made me think about life and how it slogged on and on and never stopped. Babies were born, old people died. And not just old people, because un-old people died, too. Kids, even, which of course made me think of Joseph. I grew even more depressed.

We left the mall and went to Memorial Park, where at least the sun felt good on our skin. And then, at three-thirty, we went home. I think we both felt lame.

As Sandra pulled into the driveway, my eyes flew to the front porch. It was dumb, *I* was dumb, but I couldn't help it. Ever since the day of the telephone call, I'd been hoping Lars would magically show up and make everything better. Like he did that day at the beginning of the year, when there he was, lounging against the house looking so adorable and nervous.

Lars wasn't there. My shoulders slumped.

Sandra drove around back to the garage. She parked and cut off the engine, but she didn't get out.

"Listen," she said. "What you asked earlier? About making someone love you?"

I flushed.

"Well, I need to tell you something about that, because probably you *can't* make someone love you. And if they don't, they don't, and you're better off without them."

I kept my eyes glued to the dashboard.

"Seriously, it's better to be alone than to wish you were alone," she said. "Okay?"

I appreciated her effort, but I'd never wished I was alone when I was with Lars. I'd wished Nose-Ring Girl was alone, not me.

Sandra flopped back against her seat, as if aware of how unhelpful she was being. "Or maybe that's just crap," she said. "Or maybe sometimes it's crap and sometimes it's not, depending on the situation. And Lars . . ."

Lars. His name filled me with longing.

Sandra turned her head so that she faced me. "Can I start over here? Can I try the whole advice thing again?"

"I guess," I said.

"The thing is . . . Lars is a good guy. He's just stupid. Only, you're kind of being stupid, too."

I gazed at her. This was brilliant attempt number two?

"Because one thing I do know—and I don't know a lot, but I do know this—is that you can't wallow. Wallowing will get you nowhere."

"Didn't we just spend the whole day wallowing?" I said.

"Er . . ." She looked embarrassed, then regrouped and held up her finger. "Case in point. And did it make things better?"

"Not really. But kind of."

"No, it didn't, and you know it." She exhaled. "What I'm trying to say here is that maybe you should talk to him again."

"But that would be weak."

"Maybe. Or maybe he's the one who's weak, and he needs you to take the first step." She arched her eyebrows. "But like I said, what do I know?"

Everything, I thought. *You're my big sister.*

"You really think I should talk to him?" I said. It hurt how much I wanted to.

"It can't make things any worse," she said fatalistically. "You're, like, in this state of not-knowing, and that sucks more than anything. *Probably* it's over—but if you ask him straight out, at least you'll know for sure."

"True," I said in a tiny voice. I nodded to give myself bravery. "Thanks."

•••

Stepping into our house felt like stepping back into Normal Life. Bright sunny kitchen, good clean smells, the sound of Ty acting out some drama in the den involving Ninjas. Then we heard the sound of Mom's clogs clomping down the stairs and through the living room.

Angry clomps, full of angry Mom-ness.

"Uh-oh," Sandra said.

Mom strode into the kitchen. We knew it was over by the expression on her face. "*Girls*," she said.

"Bu-sted," Sandra murmured, drawing the word out.

Mom whirled on her. "Don't you make light of this! What was going through your head, cutting an entire day of school? And not only that, but encouraging your sister—your *thirteen-year-old sister*—to follow you into your life of crime?"

"Mom," I said. "Skipping one day is hardly a—"

"Hush," she said to me. "I am not any happier with you, so you just keep your mouth shut, do you hear?"

I couldn't keep my mouth shut *and* respond to her question. But I knew I was going to lose either way, so I said, "Um . . . sorry?"

"You better be," she said. "I brought you your English paper, Winnie, because that is the kind of good mother I am. I saw it on the counter and thought, 'Oh, poor Winnie,' and I delivered it to your classroom. Only guess what?"

I shrank.

"That's right! You weren't in your classroom!" Mom said. She switched back to Sandra. "So I tried calling, but your phone went straight to voice mail. So I rushed to the administration office, thinking, 'Were they in a wreck? Are they lying maimed and dead on the road somewhere?' "

Oh good golly. Maimed and dead? I knew we'd screwed up . . . but *maimed and dead*?

"Mom," Sandra started.

Mom waggled her finger. "Oh no no. Uh-uh. And then to find out from Mrs. Westin that I myself had called in to say you'd be absent? That you had a *stomach bug*?!"

Sandra winced. I cringed. But even though we were in trouble, there was something solid about standing with Sandra as Mom's scolding rained down.

"Mom, I'm really sorry," Sandra said.

"Me, too," I piped in.

"I just . . . I don't . . ." Sandra exhaled. "It's like I'm out of control or something!"

Where was she going with this? "Me, too," I said less certainly.

"I don't even trust my own judgment anymore," Sandra continued. "All this stress about being a senior, it's gotten to me so much more than I thought. And I *know* I shouldn't have let Winnie cut. She's just an eighth grader. What was I thinking?"

I was confused. What *was* she thinking? And what was this business about me being "just an eighth grader"?

Mom sighed, and her expression went from angry to not quite as angry. "Oh, Sandra."

"I'm a mess," Sandra said, her voice quavering. "I'm a complete and total mess!"

It was as if a train was zooming past, and I better jump on it, quick. "Me, too!" I said. "An even messier mess!"

They stared at me.

The phone rang, a high-pitched trill that Ty had punched in on the menu button and that none of us could manage to change back. Mom startled, and then her features went back to being stern.

"Don't think I'm done with you two," she warned as she strode across the kitchen. She picked up the phone. "Hello? Oh, hi! How are you?"

She talked. Sandra and I eyed each other.

"I can't believe you left your English paper at home, idiot," Sandra whispered. She shoved me.

"I can't believe you blamed everything on senior stress!" I whispered in return. I shoved her back.

" 'Cause it's true! I've lost all sense of reason!" She kept her self-righteousness alive for another couple of seconds, and then she drew her knuckles to her mouth. She giggled, and so did I.

"Carol, that's wonderful!" Mom said, over by the back door. "I'm so glad to hear it. Oh, I'm just *so* glad. Thanks so much for telling me!"

"That's a lot of 'so's," Sandra commented.

"*Soooo* many," I agreed.

Mom got off the phone. She clopped back to us—happy clops this time—and her face was lit up. "That was Carol Webber, Ty's teacher. She just heard from Joseph's mom. He's turned the corner!"

"He has?" Sandra said. She hadn't gone to the hospital with us, but she knew about Joseph and had been just as worried as the rest of us.

"What does that mean?" I asked.

"It means he's responding to the treatment. His white blood cell count is going down. It looks like he's going to be okay!"

My chest clutched up. "For real? *Okay* okay, as in forever?"

Mom was teary. She smiled through it and said "That's what the doctors are saying."

A balloon opened up inside me, pushing the clutchiness away and replacing it with joy. Mom pulled me and Sandra into a hug, and we hugged her back. We were a big ball of hugginess. We pressed warm and hard together, being careful of Mom's baby bump.

"I don't know what I would do if I lost you girls," Mom murmured, her voice catching.

"Or Ty," I said.

"Or Ty." Mom squeezed tighter.

"Does this mean we're not punished?" Sandra said.

Mom released us. Beaming, she said, "Are you nuts? Of

course you're punished. You both have Saturday detentions for the next four Saturdays, and you're on kitchen duty for the rest of your lives."

Sandra groaned. She hated doing the dishes.

"She's probably too much of a mess to clean up the kitchen," I offered.

Sandra shot daggers at me. "I *am*," she said.

"Well, a tidy kitchen equals a tidy soul," Mom said gaily. "Now let's go tell Ty the good news."

Later, when I told Mom there was something I had to do and asked if I could go out for a teeny-tiny little hour before dinner, she said, "You're kidding, right?"

"Um . . . no?" I said.

"You skipped school, and you're asking if you can go out?"

"Um . . . yes?" I made praying hands. "It's really important, I swear. Or I wouldn't ask."

She regarded me.

"Please? Pleasie please please?" I was full of wheedling on the surface, doing my best to be winning and cute. But the need inside me was raw and true. "*Please*?"

She rolled her eyes. "Fine—one hour. But I don't know why I'm letting you."

" 'Cause you're the best mom ever," I said. "That's why."

As I biked to Lars's house, I didn't let myself think. I just pedaled, focusing on not letting my skirt catch in the chain. But when I got there, his dad said Lars was out with friends.

"Can you tell me where?" I asked. "It's important."

"I think he's at Bryce's," Mr. Mitchell said.

So I went to Bryce's. This wasn't part of the plan, but then again, I didn't actually have a plan. *Just* do *it*, I kept chanting to myself. *Do it, do it, do it.* I conjured up Dinah in my mind—Dinah, of all people—and reminded myself how brave she'd been the time she confronted Cinnamon. She'd said the hard thing that needed to be said. If Dinah could do it, surely I could, too.

I knocked on Bryce's door. Brianna's friend Stephanie opened it, and my stomach cramped.

She took in my head-to-toe black, and her mouth twisted. "Hello, Death."

Ha ha. I could feel my face heat up.

"Is Lars here?" I asked.

"Maybe."

"*Maybe*?" I lifted my chin and acted ballsier than I felt. "Do you think you could act like a normal person, please? Just for once?"

She faltered, then scowled and stepped aside. Lars's laugh rang out from the basement, followed by Nose-Ring Girl's giggle. Brianna's giggle—whatever. I gulped and headed downstairs.

Bryce saw me first. He glanced up in surprise and said, "Winnie—hey!"

"Hey," I replied.

Lars straightened up fast from the pool table. Brianna stood way too close to him, wearing a tight brown T-shirt and a silver choker with a star dangling from it.

"Winnie!" Lars said. "What are you doing here?"

It wasn't bad, the way he said it. In fact, he seemed happy. Hopeful, in a I'm-a-guy-and-I'm-going-to-act-cool sort of way. Brianna, on the other hand, crossed her arms over her chest and glowered. She looked like a potato.

"Can I talk to you?" I asked Lars.

"Sure," he said.

Brianna made a sound of protest. "It's your turn. You haven't taken your turn."

"It won't take long," I started to say, but I bit down on my words. I wasn't a nuisance, easily taken care of. I wasn't going to act like one.

"Take your shot," Brianna told Lars, jerking her chin at the pool table. She edged a fraction of an inch closer to him. "She can wait."

"No, I can't," I said. Just simply.

Lars looked at Brianna, whose fingers had traveled to his sleeve and grabbed hold. He looked at me. I kept my gaze level.

Lars peeled Brianna off him. He put down his cue stick and came over.

"What's up?" he said. "Why weren't you at school today? Are you sick?"

He noticed! I thought.

"No, I just . . . Sandra and I, we just didn't—" I felt Brianna and Stephanie shooting hate-rays at me. "Can we go outside?"

"Yeah," Lars said.

"Dude? The game?" Bryce said.

"You shoot for me," Lars said.

"We're on different teams!"

"Then don't."

We went to Bryce's porch, and I told him how Sandra and I had ditched. He looked impressed, which made me feel tough, and which made me forget for a moment that I wasn't. *Maybe that's why Amanda does it*, I thought, thinking of her black eyeliner and her habit of hanging out behind the cafeteria. *Because it keeps you from having to be real.*

And then I thought of Joseph, which was odd, since Joseph and Amanda had nothing in common. Except maybe they did? Or used to, before Amanda went ultra-sullen-cool? And maybe . . . I don't know. Maybe Amanda needed to remember that life didn't last forever. Maybe we all needed to remember that life didn't last forever, and that the bit of it we *did* have was a gift, which at any millisecond could be taken away.

I looked at the porch's floorboards. I didn't know *what* I was thinking, only that I wanted to be real, and I wanted to be real with Lars.

"Winnie?" he said.

I lifted my eyes to his. I'd been nervous all along, but now I got crazy-shaky nervous, my muscles twitchy and jittering.

"Um," I started. "I wanted to ask you . . ."

"Yeah?" He jammed his hands in his pockets and hunched his shoulders. Gone was his cool-boy façade, and his own nervousness buzzed off his body and combined with mine. It was nearly unbearable. Why was it so hard, sometimes, to be a human and simply exist?

"Do you *want* to be broken up?" I asked.

Lars shook his head. He blinked rapidly, and his lip trembled, and I was pretty much thrown into shock, because I'd never seen him like this before.

"*No*," he said. His shoulders shook, and I flung myself onto him. He pulled his hands out of his pockets and embraced me. He held me close, so close, and when he pulled back, I saw he was crying.

He half-laughed and said, "These are very manly tears. You know that, right?"

"Oh, yeah," I said. "Of course."

He took my hands and grew solemn. His Adam's apple jumped, and I knew an apology was coming. "Winnie . . ."

I almost cut him off, because my chest was ballooning again, and I wanted him to know it was okay. It was *so* okay. But some secret strong part of me said, *No. Let him.*

"I was a jerk," he said. "A phenomenally huge jerk, and I don't deserve someone as wonderful as you."

"You got that right," I said.

He looked straight at me. "And I'm sorry."

"Well . . ." I could drag it out, but why? I was ready to start fresh. That's what the real me wanted to do.

"Okay, I forgive you," I said. I grinned, and a smile like a flower opened on his face. A flower of the manliest sort.

Later that evening, I shared my happiness with Ty. Lars had wanted to take me out for ice cream (it *was* Valentine's Day, after all), but I turned him down, knowing I had something else I needed to take care of. Plus, I was technically still in the doghouse with Mom, and I knew there was no way she was going to let me go out a second time. For dinner she'd made lasagna, which involved lots of pans and utensils and dried-up-sauciness, and she was hummingly gleeful as she flitted about making a mess.

"Thanks, girls," she said to me and Sandra at the end of the meal. She rose with Dad to retire to the sun porch. "The lasagna dish needs hand washing—don't forget!"

But the cleanup didn't last forever, and by seven-thirty I was in the basement with Ty, watching *Pirates of the Caribbean: Dead Man's Chest.*

Ty snuggled beside me on the sofa for a while, then squirmed and kicked at the fuzzy throw we'd wrapped around ourselves. He shifted positions, putting his head on a sofa cushion and his feet in my lap. He farted.

"Ty! Pew," I said, pulling away and fanning the air.

He giggled. "Sorry." He wiggled up closer, pressing his jeans against my thigh, and I thought how lovely it was that it took so little to make things right between us again.

"Don't you dare stink again," I said. "I will spank you."

"You are not allowed to spank," he said.

"Tough. If you stink on my leg, I will spank you and throw you in the hold of Davy Jones's boat."

He giggled some more. Will, the cuter of the movie's two heroes, was currently trapped in the hold of Davy Jones's boat, and it wasn't good. Davy Jones was an undead pirate with tentacles dripping from his face and two slits for a nose.

"Hey, Winnie?" Ty said. He twisted on the pillow to look at me.

"Huh?"

"Have you had a mainly happy life?"

His question took me by surprise. I wondered if it had to do with Joseph, with sadnesses that could have been, but weren't.

"Yeah, I guess," I said. "Have you?"

"Aye-aye, cap'n," he said. "Mainly."

I hugged him, dodgy bottom and all.

March

MAGNOLIA GRACE PERRY burst into the world on a drizzly Saturday afternoon, two weeks before her due date and three days before my fourteenth birthday. If she'd waited three more days—only three more days!—we'd have been birthday twins, which I once thought would have been horrible. But now there was a part of me that thought it could have been cool, like a sign from God or something.

Then again, we'd have had to share parties till the end of time, which could have potentially sucked. When Maggie turned one, it wouldn't have mattered, since one-year-olds didn't even know what birthdays are. But when she turned two and actually had opinions? No way was I having a "My Little Pony" party, and I doubted she'd be too psyched about having a "Yay, I got my driver's license!" party.

So maybe God knew what he was doing after all.

How weird that I'd be getting my driver's license in only two years!

Sandra drove me and Ty to the hospital as soon as Dad called with the news. The rain stopped as we pulled up in front of the main entrance, and above the building we saw a rainbow. True. Forever and ever, part of Maggie's story would be that we saw a rainbow on the day she was born.

I remembered how to get to the elevators from the time Ty and I came to visit Joseph, so I led the way. The maternity ward was more cheerful than the pediatric ward, the lounges populated with fat ol' mommies and fat ol' mommies-to-be. There were proud grandparents and nervous new dads. One dad was passing out chocolate cigars, which reminded me of a Hallmark special, and when I grinned at him, he bounded over and gave me one. He gave cigars to Sandra and Ty, too, since it would have been impolite not to.

There were doctors and supply carts and a hospital volunteer delivering flowers. And, of course, there were babies.

Maggie was the cutest of them all.

"Hey there," Mom said when the three of us burst into her room. She smiled wearily. Nestled to her chest was a puff of blanket, and, sticking out from the top, a teeny sucking red face.

"She's nursing," Mom explained.

Ty stepped closer, fascinated. "Did I do that?"

"You sure did," Dad said. If Mom looked tired, Dad looked downright exhausted, even though he wasn't the one who'd given birth. Later, he'd no doubt make it sound like he had. When Mom was in labor with Sandra, Dad had offered her an ice chip, and Mom had thrown a hairbrush at him. That was part of Sandra's story. With Maggie, the whole of her details had yet to pour forth. But they would.

"You were a breastfeeding champ," Dad told Ty. "You about sucked your mother dry."

"*Da-a-d*," Sandra said. I agreed.

"You did not," Mom reassured Ty. She gestured to all of us. "Come here. Come meet your baby sister."

Maggie must have sensed that something important was happening, because she stopped nursing and gazed up at us. Her eyes were dark and murky, the color of a swamp.

"She's beautiful," Sandra said. There was a note of wistfulness in her voice, and I wondered if it was hard for her, knowing that she'd be off and gone to college before Maggie took her first step or said her first word. It was hard for me, knowing Sandra would be gone. But I'd tell Maggie all about her. I'd teach her the same stuff Sandra had taught me.

Omigosh. I hadn't thought of it like this, but I'd be Maggie's Sandra. Only I'd be less Sandra-ish and more Winnie-ish, and when Maggie grew up she'd thank her stars for her lovely good fortune. Tee hee.

"She's so cute," Ty said. "Even though she's bald. She's a bald, bald cutie."

Mom sat up and pulled shut her gown. She kissed Maggie's button nose, then said to Ty, "Do you want to hold her?"

Ty did. He sat on a chair by Mom's side, and Mom handed Maggie to Dad, who placed her in Ty's arms.

"Watch her head," Dad said, showing Ty how to support Maggie so that her neck didn't bobble. She was wrapped in the same hospital-issue blanket I remembered from when Ty was born. It was white with pink and blue stripes, which I thought was clever. That way it worked for girl babies and boy babies, both.

Ty held Maggie for about thirty seconds, then announced, "I'm done. You hold her, Winnie. And then Sandra, so it'll be youngest to oldest."

I lifted the Maggie-bundle from Ty's lap. I didn't need Dad's help. I cradled her in my arms and said, "Hey, sweet teensy. You smell good."

Ty hopped up. "I want to smell! I want to smell!"

"Relax," Sandra told him as I twisted away protectively. "You already had your turn."

"But I didn't smell her," he complained.

"You'll be smelling her plenty, I promise you," Sandra said. "Maybe she smells good now, but just wait."

"Till what?" Ty said.

"Till she poops," Sandra said.

"Oh, man," Dad said. "Talk about poopy babies—Sandra, you nearly blasted my hair off the first time I changed your diaper."

"The *only* time you changed her diaper," Mom said.

On it went, the teasing discussion of Ty's favorite subject and as they teased each other, I walked with Maggie to the hospital window. The maternity ward was on the fifth floor. From where we stood, we could see sidewalks and trees and streets.

Well, I could. Maggie probably couldn't. Her eyes were too new.

"That's the world down there," I said softly. "Isn't it pretty?"

She cooed, and I thought of all that awaited her: her whole life, stretching out even further than the busy Atlanta streets.

"Oh, little Mags," I whispered, bringing her cheek to mine. "I have so much to tell you."